O9-BTM-786

DISCOVERING EVE

DISCOVERING EVE

SHORT STORIES

JANE CANDIA COLEMAN

SWALLOW PRESS / OHIO UNIVERSITY PRESS

Swallow Press/Ohio University Press books are printed on acid-free paper ∞

Library of Congress Cataloging-in-Publication Data

Coleman, Jane Candia.
Discovering Eve : short stories / Jane Candia Coleman.
p. cm.
ISBN 0-8040-0964-3
1. Women—Fiction. I. Title.
PS3553.047427D57 1993
813′.54—dc20 92-37638
CIP

"The Balducci Garden" appeared in *The Pennsylvania Review.*

"Freddy, The Blind Professor and the Scent of Roses" appeared in *Playgirl* as "Things That Touch the Heart."

"The Lover of Swamps" appeared in *The Agassiz Review.*

"Compromising Alice" appeared in *Crosscurrents.*

"The Age of Insects" appeared in *Blue Moon,* and received First Prize for fiction in 1987.

"The Laborer in the Vineyard" appeared in *The Uncommon Reader.*

"Wives and Lovers" appeared in *Sewickley Magazine,* and received First Prize for fiction in 1985.

"La Signora Julia" appeared in *Antietam Review.*

FOR LEAH WITH LOVE . . .

TABLE OF CONTENTS

PART I

THE BALDUCCI GARDEN

THE BALDUCCI GARDEN

POMPEO AND FABIO BALDUCCI lived next door to my grandmother in a house with a large walled garden. In it were paths and beds of fruit and flowers, and grottoes where plaster cherubs held out clusters of grapes; where turtles, frogs, and even, I remember, a goose, seemed frozen in sunlight. And there was a deep and quiet pool spanned by a bridge, a single curve of concrete over the water, that was high enough so you could sit dangling your legs and watching the glimmer of goldfish beneath white lilies.

The Balducci brothers were bachelors and as retiring as rabbits, though we all knew that Fabio had been engaged for many years to Renata, a friend of my aunt's, and that a marriage was imminent. It never happened, though, that marriage, and, during the summer that I was ten, I thought I had discovered why.

My cousins and I were not encouraged to visit in the garden. It was a peculiarly adult place, laid out for peace and visual pleasure, and the brothers sat in it sipping coffee, or worked there on summer evenings, secure behind their wall.

Sometimes Fabio would sing, unleashing a clear, golden tenor voice that lifted and fell and underscored things I was looking at so they became important, linked in my mind by the flight of song.

The Balduccis were musicians, set apart from the rest of us by their ability to transpose feeling into music. Looking back, I suppose that neither had a great gift, certainly not of the caliber that would insure fame yet large enough to let them live with a certain elegance. Pompeo played piano and organ in the church, and gave music lessons on Saturday mornings. My cousins had all, at one time or another, been under his spell, but in the summer that I was ten only Carlotta had progressed far enough to be preparing for a recital. Carlotta studied voice, too, with Fabio, and she wanted to be in the movies. She practiced diligently, hour after hour, first the piano and then the songs which she offered in a high, nasal soprano so unlike Fabio's tenor as to be painful.

"Huh!" my mother said. "With a face like that she'll be lucky to get a husband, never mind the movies."

It was true. Carlotta was plain. Her hair was thin and mouse-colored, and she had spots on her face that never left her, just moved, it seemed, from one place to another.

When she finished practicing, she would go to her room that I shared when I visited, and she would smooth cold cream into her cheeks and over her arms and legs as diligently as she had played and sung.

"An actress has to take care of her skin," she said to me, both hands around one pale leg and stroking upward from ankle to thigh. "Skin is important."

Though at first she tried to be friends, I thought she was boring, and I thought the makeup she put on her face and eyes looked ridiculous. But Carlotta was in love with Fabio, and that set her apart, gave her the right to preen and stroke herself, to treat me as if I were still a child.

Each year, when Fabio's marriage to Renata was put off, she grew more certain that he was waiting for her to grow up.

"We'll go to New York," she said that summer. "We'll be stars. He told me I could be a star if I work hard enough."

I thought about that. It didn't seem possible. I knew what "stars" looked like, and it wasn't like Carlotta with her no-colored hair and eyes that disappeared behind thick glasses. I left her, wrapped in self-concern, and went to find the boy cousins who were oblivious to their older sister's dreaming.

That was the summer that we, the boys and I, discovered that rocks had hearts; glistening, crystalline centers patterned and colored as surely as any kaleidoscope and in as many variations. In the backyard, next to the grape arbor, was a huge outcrop of stone too big to be removed, too hard to be leveled without dynamite. It was a presence. The house, the garden flowed around it, took it into account, left it alone. We used it as a stage for our plays, and as a tool, an implacable surface upon which we hurled the stones we collected, hurling them time and time again until they cracked, shattered, exposed themselves and their shining cores.

In the mornings we set out into the fields pulling wagons that we loaded with carefully selected stones and slowly hauled home. Single-minded as ants or bees, we trudged back and forth along the leafy lanes where the sand glittered with mica and the summer weeds grew taller than our heads and shaded us in our labors.

It was on one of these excursions that I discovered that the wall behind the Balducci house was crumbling, that I could climb it and enter the garden at will without invitation or anyone's knowledge. I kept the fact secret, like a gift that I would open when the time was right.

Each afternoon after lunch, if my mother was visiting or merely sitting lazily under the arbor drinking coffee with my aunts and gossiping, and therefore too occupied to take me to the beach, the boys and I would begin our assault on the stones.

Even now I am not sure where my fascination lay; whether it was in my power to break apart stone, or in the manifestation of the hidden beauty, the swirling and tangible shapes that lay beneath ordinary surfaces. I think that it was the latter; the idea that what was secret was lovely beyond all my imaginings; that there were in the world all kinds of mysteries waiting to be discovered. Behind the whispers of adults, behind closed doors and walls, lay a world shaken by beauty, and I had only to find the crack to enter.

I began, shamelessly, to eavesdrop. I became adept at spying, at coming and going noiselessly, at sitting motionless in the corner of my grandmother's kitchen listening to the talk that flowed there like wine. For sooner or later everyone came to her kitchen. Sometimes it seemed as if the whole town was there nibbling cookies, drinking coffee from the pot on the stove that, magically, was never empty.

The kitchen was a long room of perhaps fifty feet, and below the rest of the house, which was reached by stairs in one corner. How often I sat on those stairs in the dark, listening to adult conversations. Much of it was in Italian that I strained to understand but never did except for a word here and there. It was mostly the men who spoke it, my grandfather's and my uncle's friends, and their talk was of politics, business, the making of money, things not nearly as interesting as the women's gossip. I learned from them that Aunt Rhea, Carlotta's mother, had entrapped Uncle Carlo into marriage, just how I wasn't sure, and that he now had a woman in town; that Iole, the woman next door, had female troubles; and that, in all probability, Fabio would never marry Renata.

"What's the matter with them?" my Aunt Mary asked. "Why don't they just get on with it?"

"Maybe he doesn't want to. Or maybe she's waiting for somebody better."

"Better!" Aunt Mary said. "What's better? You tell me."

"Anyway," my mother said, "if you can get the milk, why buy the cow?"

I imagined her as she spoke, leaning back in her chair sleek and sure of herself, passing sentence as she alone could do, and blowing smoke from her nose.

"Ah," said my grandmother, sitting down with them, "who can ever say what's in the mind of a woman? Or a man."

Above our heads, in the living room, Carlotta began her scales. "La, la, la, la," she sang, her voice breaking into a shriek on the high notes.

"Again?" said my mother. "How can you stand it?"

"Poverina," my grandmother said. "She has to have something. What can I do?"

"Tell her to stop."

"Let her have her dreams," said my grandmother. "It will pass, and when she gets married I'll give her my gold necklace."

"Married?" said my mother. "Who'll have her? And what about Maria? She's your granddaughter, too."

"Greedy," my grandmother said to her. "Always you're the greedy one. The garnet bracelets. Those are for her."

Garnet bracelets. For me. Dark red jewels to flash on my arm as surely as the rock crystals flashed in stone. I dreamed about them, red as drops of blood.

Carlotta said, "When I'm a star I'll have a diamond tiara and a fox stole."

I pictured diamonds in her lifeless hair. "That's dumb," I said. I was in bed under the sheet. She was in front of the mirror creaming her face and fussing with a spot on her chin. She looked at me in the glass.

"Why?" she demanded.

"Because it is," I said.

"When I'm famous I won't speak to you," she said. "I'll walk right past you on the street and never even look at you. Or your stuck-up mother."

"Don't you talk about my mother," I said, sitting up in bed. "And don't you snub her, either."

"She thinks I won't make it," Carlotta said, glaring at me. "She thinks she's so smart. But I will make it. I will."

"She is smart. And pretty, too. And our house is nicer than yours."

"I'm going to have a swimming pool," she said. "And servants. And they won't let you in. I'll have Fabio. And a dining room with a skylight. And a big bed. And we'll . . ." She looked at me and laughed. "Never mind," she said. "You're too little. You wouldn't understand."

I thought I would, though. She and Fabio would kiss in there, hold on to each other the way grownups did. I thought about Fabio; about him kissing Carlotta. "Don't be disgusting," I said. I pulled the sheet over my head and lay there waiting for her to turn out the light.

She crawled into her bed. "That proves it," she said. She arranged her head, bristling with curlers, on her pillow. "You're still a baby. You don't know anything about love."

I was sure that love was beautiful. What I didn't know was how you knew it when it came, what you did that proved it. How was Carlotta so sure of Fabio? How did they all seem to know things, all the women, while I didn't? What door had I to go through, what rock break apart, before I, too, was initiated?

Waking, the garnets continued to haunt me. I wanted to see them but couldn't ask without admitting that I had listened, so I continued smashing stones, lost in something not quite of the world.

After a time the boys lost interest. They had their baseball games, their swimming, other friends, and so I went on alone, lugging stones and sometimes slipping into the Balducci's garden where I sat looking quietly down upon the pond where the goldfish quivered like streaks of sunlight.

It happened, of course, that one day I was alone with my grandmother. Carlotta was practicing. My mother had gone to lunch after an hour spent fluffing her hair, powdering her nose, tweezing her eyebrows into arcs. I was allowed to watch the transformation but never to talk. As a reward she had rouged my cheeks, painted my mouth with lipstick.

"Clown face," my grandmother said. She was rolling pasta on the big kitchen table. Back and forth her arms went, moving the rolling pin with competence. Back and forth. And the white dough spread, thinned, shone under her knife as she cut it into strips that she hung to dry on two long sticks suspended between chair backs. Her felt slippers slapped the floor as she moved. Flour dusted her hands, her hair, rising in a silvery cloud that made her stop suddenly and sneeze.

"Be a good girl," she said. "Upstairs. In my bureau. Bring me a handkerchief."

I went, skirting Carlotta at the piano and entering my grandmother's bedroom. There was a high carved bed there covered with a woven spread. And a rocking chair. And a gilt crucifix on the wall above the bed. There was a huge chest with a glass over it. The glass was old, greenish, filled with tiny specks and irregularities so my reflection wavered as I opened the top drawer. Inside were silver hair combs and pins for her chignon. A box of buttons, perhaps a thousand of them, all sizes, shapes, colors, none seeming to match. I took a handful. They shone in my palm. There was a box of thread, too, and a gold thimble, and a pincushion like a strawberry. There was a prayer book and a rosary of amber beads, and prayer cards, one with a pink and blue virgin, the other of the Sacred Heart. It was a large red heart entwined with thorns, and the valves and veins showed on the outside. I looked at it a long time, afraid to touch it, frightened by its realism. Beside it lay a fan, its handle yellow ivory like piano keys.

It was then that I remembered the garnets and began searching the drawers, through folded petticoats, blouses, stockings neatly rolled in pairs. I found the box beneath a pile of shawls. Inside lay the gold necklace with its long, heavy links, and a pair of earrings like teardrops. And the garnet bracelets, three strands each, dark and hard looking against the worn velvet. I put them on. The necklace, too. I looked in the glass. A woman looked back at me, dark eyed with dark hair and rouge on her cheeks.

"Good afternoon," I said. "How lovely to see you."

She smiled. "And you," she said. "And you."

"Madam," I said, "please try these earrings. They would suit you."

She did, screwing them gently into place, tilting her head in concentration.

"Oh, lovely," I said. "Perfect."

We nodded again, smiled, swept closer to each other gracefully. I snapped open the fan. Oh, it was a splendid sight!

"What're you doing with my necklace?" Carlotta hissed from the doorway, her neck extended like a goose. "Give me that!"

She snatched at me, tearing an earring loose.

"Leave me alone," I said.

"Sneak!" she said. "Always sneaking around. I'm telling."

"Nonna told me to come in here." I clutched at the necklace.

"Not to try on her stuff, she didn't. I'm telling anyhow. Wait'll your mother hears."

"Nobody told *you* to come in here, either," I said. I struggled to keep back tears. When my mother heard, she'd be furious. She always insisted that I behave when I was here, that I show them how well brought up I was, and what a lady.

"Children, children," my grandmother said. Then she saw me. "Ah, bellissima," she said. "That's what you're doing."

"She sneaked in," Carlotta said. "She's playing with your things."

"Basta, basta," she said to her. "She's little. She didn't mean anything."

Carlotta gave me a look of pure hate. You wait, it said. You wait.

I let the tears come. I buried my face in my grandmother's soft and yielding bosom that smelled of flour and talcum powder. She patted me. "Don't cry, " she said. "Those bracelets are for you when you grow up. And the necklace," she said to Carlotta, "the necklace is for you. But you have to be good girls. No fighting."

I nodded, still buried in darkness. I didn't think Carlotta would forget and be good. I had a hunch she'd bring it up at the dinner table, embarrass me in front of them all. She'd done it before, to me and to the boys. It was her way of drawing attention to herself, as if her music wasn't enough, as if she had to be a person, too, and not just the hands and voice that dominated the upstairs.

"Pray to Jesus, both of you," my grandmother said. "Now put these away, and no more fighting. No tears." She patted me on the head. "Get yourself a handkerchief."

Then she went slowly downstairs. I could hear the pad of her slippers and then the clatter of the rolling pin. I found the earring that had dropped, put everything back in place, and closed the drawer. I didn't want to have to pass by Carlotta, but I had to. I went out into the living room.

"Piss pot," she said to me.

I couldn't think of a worse word except one . The one I wasn't supposed to say, *ever.* "Fucker," I said, and saying it felt good as if something inside had broken loose. I laughed. "That's what you are." I hopped down the stairs.

But I grew restless in the kitchen, and hot. My grandmother had turned on the radio and was listening to the opera, sometimes singing along, and I was tired of music, of the constant pouring out of people's feelings. In the yard cicadas whirred; the leaves in the grape arbor stirred and rustled and made patterns on the terrace. I opened the screen door and went out.

I played with my stones awhile, rearranging them in piles. I picked at the crystals until some fell and lay shining in my hand. Sweat collected under my hair at the back of my neck. It was a perfect day for swimming, for being at the beach, but there was no one to take me, no one, even, to talk to.

I got up, walked toward the woods, then climbed the wall into the Balducci's garden. I moved cautiously toward the pond. The brothers weren't at home during the day, but you never knew. I dabbled my feet in the water, but it was warm, stagnant, with a floating green weed that wrapped around my ankles. It was so hot that even the fish were still, resting on the bottom so I could see only their outlines, the faint ripple of their fins.

The stone goose reminded me of Carlotta, but the turtle, wide-backed and mossy, let me sit on him awhile. I leaned back on my hands and looked at the sky, a clear and burning blue. One cloud stood motionless over my head.

I froze when I heard the car, the spatter of gravel under tires. Through the leaves I saw Renata's little car stop by the side of the house. I saw her emerge, like a bright butterfly from a cocoon; long, tanned legs and feet in open-toed white shoes, a yellow skirt that swirled around her like wings or petals, a ruffled blouse, and that hair, that red-gold Italian hair.

I saw Fabio greet her at the door, his hair a darker version of hers, more like bronze, and tightly curled. They went inside and the door clicked shut.

I sat awhile longer, watching the cloud that refused to move, and then I grew restless again, drawn to the house as surely as if pulled on a string, as if a spell were on me, on the afternoon that droned and clattered with the rubbing of insect wings.

They weren't in the kitchen or the dining room, one glance showed that. Beyond was the living room, a long, sunken space with a fireplace and a huge brass chandelier, and two couches facing one another. It was always a dark room, even in midday. Ivy clung to the casement windows, persistent, green, casting shadows. I peeked in. I had caught them, I thought, in an argument. Their words hung almost visible in the air. Renata had her head thrown back. Above the ruffled neck of her blouse, her breasts swelled, heaving as if in anger. Fabio's hands were stretched out toward them. While I watched they moved, as sinuously as the goldfish, came to rest upon her breasts and curved around them, and her anger seemed to fade, to metamorphose into a different fire. The corners of her mouth twitched in a quick smile. She took a step toward him, forcing herself more deeply into his hands. When he pulled the blouse from her shoulders, I saw that she was naked underneath, that her breasts were huge and white with nipples so dark they didn't seem to belong. He lowered his mouth to them, one and then the other, while she stood, still with her head thrown back, laughing.

As if I were watching a play or a painting come to life I watched them kissing, touching one another, removing their clothes so that each was revealed. She, lush, white as marble, with curved haunches like a mare's, and he like a statue, mounting, riding her away while she tossed under him still laughing.

When they had finished they lay still as if asleep or drugged by the heat, and I sat down under the window breathing hard. My stomach ached, and I didn't want to move, for moving would break something in me, would tear at the fragile core of my body until I bled.

This was what they whispered about, those women with their thin and whiplike tongues; what they did behind closed doors in the night, in the afternoon, with their husbands, their men, with my father and grandfather. It was what they meant when they said, half in sorrow, half in jest, "You'll be married, too, someday," and laughed their hard, meaningful laughter. This was what Aunt Rhea had done, and Uncle Carlo's woman in town.

This was what Carlotta dreamed of—she and Fabio in their house, their bed. Only dreams did not come true, at least not this one for her. I saw it as clearly as I had seen Fabio and Renata. Carlotta would never star, never have this bronzed creature of her dreams. Like the rest of them she would marry, go behind a closed door, and what she held in her heart would be hidden as the core of a stone.

My own heart ached, and my stomach twisted. I would have to go back, to the house, the kitchen, and they would be there, all of them, female like me, no longer different, no longer secret, not any part, and I would have to smile at them, the small, flickering smile of knowledge I had seen on Renata's bold face, and keep hidden what I knew of the menace, the inexpressible beauty of love.

FREDDY, THE BLIND PROFESSOR, AND THE SCENT OF ROSES

THE SUMMER I was twenty I had a job reading sociology texts to a blind professor. I went to his office every afternoon at one o'clock precisely, hurrying over the heated pavement to his dim little cell as if it were a kind of sanctuary, which it was.

Within its walls the happenings of the world took on a new perspective; one's senses were reversed, and perception took place through what seemed like layers of water or planes of light, a distance not physical but induced by the man within. It was a room of shadows until I arrived and raised the shades to read. It was a place of silence until my words echoed there.

The professor was a gentle man but often irritated by noise and the harshness of voices. Since sound was his way of seeing, he tried to control what came to him, and he made me aware of my voice as I read, of its pitch, tone, quality.

"You're getting too high," he'd say. "Drop down! Drop down!"

And I'd lower my voice until it became like a cello, singing a deep, dark song that flowed out into the room and hummed around the legs of chairs like the sun rays that fell upon my lap and illuminated the pages of the book.

I would focus on making words into music, imagining my body as guitar, cello, violin, a vibrating membrane that communicated through the ear, the emotions.

The books were ponderous and dull, of no interest to me except as a score to be orchestrated. Reading them became a game that I played with fervor, sometimes forgetting the professor's presence on the chair across from mine until, like a metronome, he would catch me in musical flight.

"Slower!" he would say. "Again, please. Slowly." And he would lean forward to catch a statistic, an innuendo glossed over by my swift interpretation.

It was not a job without strain. When I left him I would be both restless and enervated, tired of words yet needing them for release. Often, instead of taking the bus, I walked home along the shaded side streets looking at lawns, trees, the flush of evening behind the hills. Sometimes I went to my friend Isabel's. If I went home I had to disclose what had transpired in the professor's office to my mother who was a great conjurer of sexual innuendo.

She feared for my virginity in that office, the two of us alone, intimate. "He's blind, for God's sake!" I said to her once, and she responded, "You'd better make sure of that." It was as if, to us both, blindness equated with impotence, proof of the state of innocence my mother lived in and never lost, and with which she tried to surround me for my safety.

Isabel and I would go out for hamburgers and then sit on her porch drinking beer, smoking, and talking with the ease of the childhood friends we were.

Sometimes her mother Maggie, a widow, would sit with us giggling, gossiping, asking me questions about "my professor," as if she, too, thought a romance was imminent. The three of us would watch as Isabel's younger sister, June, preened and took off with one or the other of the boys she was dating. Here, too, the world was at a distance, with we three women isolated, out of time and dreaming.

Maggie, however, appeared on the porch one evening as June was leaving for a party, and she looked at Isabel and me. "You go, too," she said. "Liza can stay overnight. You never know when you'll meet somebody."

Isabel and I looked at each other. "Why not?" she said. "It's better than sitting here."

I wasn't good at parties. I was shy, unable to go through the necessary convolutions of small talk. But I was always hopeful. Hope had gotten me through adolescence. I knew that someday I'd find *him,* the man meant for me, who would fall instantly in love, knowing all the good things I was too fearful to exhibit. Maggie was right. You never knew.

"Okay," I said. "Why not?"

The party was in Freddy's gameroom where he had a party every night. His parents drank heavily, and, with the callousness of alcoholics, gave him cases of beer and unlimited use of the bottom floor and the garden beyond in exchange for being left alone.

The only person I knew there was Jeff Wills. He was handsome and kind, and he sat with me at the bar drinking, asking me about myself, my job, and making me feel wanted. At one point, teasing, he gave me a whirl on the stool and I toppled off, squealing and giddy, into Freddy's arms.

Even upside down Freddy was beautiful. He had dark eyes and golden hair. Not that yellow fluff that looks like cotton thread, but real gold. It fell over his forehead as he bent to kiss me, and shone in the dim light like the hair of a nineteenth-century poet. I was a poet myself, and a romantic, and sprawled there unromantically on my back, I lost my heart.

Somehow I extricated my legs from the stool. I was on the floor kissing him and lost in it, just like I had dreamed would happen.

In the distance I heard June shouting, "Save Liza! We have to save Liza!" And I wondered why I needed to be saved, those kisses were so sweet.

Freddy kept one arm around me and pushed June away with the

other. "Be gone, Amazon!" he said theatrically and in a deep voice. "Get away!"

June was a big girl, nearly six feet tall, with what Isabel and I termed "tele-pole legs." She also had blonde hair, blue eyes, perfect teeth, and at least five boyfriends. I kissed harder.

Freddy got up pulling me with him. "Let's get out of here," he said in my ear.

We went through the door into the garden. In the dark the flowers were invisible, yet they pulsed with scent, heavy and sweet, making a pool we pushed through as if we were drugged. And we were, our senses rearranged so that touch was uppermost and speech only small sounds in the night.

For a whole summer I dreamed about those roses, woke with their scent on my clothes, my arms, can never, even now, walk past a garden of them without stopping to remember.

But memory is a fickle instrument. It dips and swoops, glosses over much, delineates what, to it, is treasure. In memory, then, it seems that for a whole summer Freddy and I hardly spoke. Perhaps we were afraid, or perhaps lost in the power of magic. In memory it is the professor who spoke, and I who gathered his words.

With the wisdom of hindsight, I can say that I was in love with love, with the romance inherent in silence. The benediction of Freddy's gaze at my face, my breasts, was enough. I felt that he worshipped, and I worshipped in return. We held on to each other as if without touch we would cease to be, as if we had created each other. Inside the breath of roses, the lonely rich kid became a man, the girl a woman who loved. And in that becoming was loveliness.

I couldn't explain any of this to Isabel when we were back in her room getting ready for sleep. Quite clearly I can remember falling onto the bed and closing my eyes, but no confidences between us.

"Well?" she said the next day, her eyes round and blue. "What happened? What's he like?"

"He's wonderful, " I said. We were sunning ourselves on her porch, and I was staring at the sky as if I, myself, had been blind and was seeing it for the first time.

"That's not what I mean . What'd he do? What'd he say? Are you going to see him again? "

Up to now we had always told each other everything, what there was of it. Now I said, "I don't know. I can't tell you."

She nodded in that way she had as if she were issuing a Papal Bull. "You must be in love with him," she said.

"I am in love with him." It felt right having said it, as if speaking made it fact.

June came out then with her hair in rollers. She was carrying a bottle of red nail polish, and she plopped down on the glider and began to paint her toe nails.

"That was rotten," she said to me. "Freddy was my date. I've been trying to get him for months."

I stared at her, at her foot propped up on the arm. I'd never gotten any boy in my life, and there she sat, painting her size ten feet and scolding me.

"Amazon," I said with relish.

She took an appraising look at her foot. "You'll never keep him," she said.

Isabel said, "Why don't you shut up? She's in love."

"Huh!" said June. "Love."

"Why don't you both shut up?" I asked. I was remembering gentle hands and breath as soft as wings.

The roar of a motor shook me out of reverie.

"He's here!" Isabel whispered. "My God, Liza! He's here!"

June tore the curlers out of her hair and ran to the steps. "Hi, Fred," she yelled.

Isabel poked me. "Get up! Get up for God's sake! He's looking for you."

I got up slowly like I was underwater, and went to the edge of the porch.

"Hi, beautiful. Come for a ride?" he said.

I didn't answer, just glided down the steps and into the front seat.

We drove into the park, kissing at stoplights and at corners, and staring at each other in between the way I had stared at the sky.

Finally he said, "What do you do besides being wonderful?"

I looked at him, tanned, broad-shouldered, golden as the Cretan bull, and awe rose in me. All by myself I had won this creature, this male who told me I was wonderful, an object of desire.

"I write poetry," I answered, knowing that to be a poet was different, was Bohemian, and therefore filled with more than ordinary middle-class passion. It was a come-on the equal of his, and he loved it.

" 'Wild nights, wild nights,' " he quoted, reaching over to touch my breast. " 'Might I but moor tonight . . . in thee.' "

I thought I'd burst with my own desire.

"You are coming back tonight, aren't you?" he asked.

I hadn't thought that far. "I guess," I answered, not wanting to sound eager. But I knew that nothing would keep me away, that I needed those moments in the garden even more than he.

"Who is the boy?" my mother asked, her suspicions aroused.

"Just a boy," I said.

"Why is he so important you have to go out two nights in a row?"

"It's fun," I answered. "I get tired working all afternoon."

"He should come and pick you up," she said. "You're chasing him, and he's not for you."

That was how she ended most of her statements, with a kind of psychological evil eye. It had always worked, and the notion that it could again frightened me. I took a long bath, washed my hair, touched perfume to my throat and between my breasts the way the beauty columns said to do. Then I put on a shirt that unzipped in front.

"So beautiful," Freddy said, freeing my breasts in the dark.

I accepted his awe as I accepted the fact that he found me beautiful without question and as if I needed to do no more than reveal myself to be loved.

And so the summer moved. Days of droning in the professor's office where the furniture was placed just so; where I sat stiff in my chair, and he sat motionless, listening with his head cocked to one side, sightless eyes fastened on nothing but sometimes on my face as if that, too, were nothing. And evenings in Freddy's arms learning a different language, lost in it and in the silence of the roses.

"Your voice is different," the professor said one day, leaning toward me as if trying to see.

"Is it?" I said. I wondered if, with those sharpened other senses, he could hear the echoes of night.

"It's richer," he said. "Easy to listen to."

He stood up and groped for his cane which I put into his hand. "Let's take a walk," he said.

We did that sometimes when he got tired of consigning to memory, or when my voice cracked with strain. We'd go out along the summer streets and he'd ask me what I saw, and I had to think a long time before telling him because he couldn't comprehend colors or even things like clouds or distance. I had to speak in similes of shapes and sounds, and, in a way, this part of the job made up for the rest.

Sometimes we would go to a coffee shop, a small place frequented by poets who read their work, which he liked, and by artists whose paintings hung on the walls and which I tried to describe to him. He would order a cappuccino for me, an espresso for himself, or sometimes tea that came in a blue-flowered pot and that had a scent as redolent as Freddy's garden.

That is what he ordered that day, and as I sniffed it with sensual pleasure, he, with his quick senses, said, "You like it. The smell."

"Mmmm," I said. "It's like a garden I know."

"Where is it? Is it yours? Describe it to me."

"It belongs to the boy I go with. It smells like roses and lavender. Like potpourri. Especially at night. You can't believe it at night."

He sipped his tea, looking toward my face and not quite connecting. "This boy. Is he special to you?"

"Yes," I said. "Oh, yes." I was still not capable of talking about Freddy. I only wrote about him in poems.

"I see," he said. Nothing more, just, "I see." A strange phrase for a blind man, but for some reason comforting. I felt that he did see, that he understood what was happening to me and, unlike others, passed no judgement.

I began to like him more after that day, to look forward to our sessions, our slow walks through the streets. I tried harder to summon up ways to describe what I was seeing. Because the world came alive for me at night, I spilled it out for the professor during the day in streams of sensual delight—leaves, blades of grass, fruit, neon signs, those peculiar tubelike structures pulsing with light that I remember I likened to arteries one could feel with one's fingers, read like Braille.

The simile delighted him. He nodded so that his hair fell over his face making him look rakish for a moment.

"Someday," he said, "I'd like you to read me your poems. Would you?"

At that time in my life I had a horror of showing my work, a fear of vulnerability that I was not to conquer for years. "I don't know," I answered. "They're not very good really." And then, afraid that I had insulted him, "When I have one that's good enough, I will."

"How will you know?"

I didn't have the answer, but in my mind I pictured a kind of unfolding, a shape I could hold in my hands. "I just will," I said.

He made a noise that could have been a chuckle. He never laughed, only sometimes gave a dry-sounding snort, as if he had no tears.

"Don't be so hard on yourself," he said. "Learn to go slowly. Learn to listen." He tightened his grip on my elbow. "Can you hear the afternoon? The light? Close your eyes."

I had never thought of listening to light, but I did as I was told. I closed my eyes and stood on the sidewalk listening. I heard leaf rustle, the grinding of cicadas, the rush of traffic, the chatter of voices, and the fall of light, warm and somnolent on my face. It sounded like honey looks in a jar, in the sun, like the scent of roses swelling like a tide.

"How strange the world is," I said, my eyes still shut. I could hear his breath, slow and steady.

"There are many facets to everything," he said. "Even to people. Especially to them." Then he moved forward and we went on threading our way through crowds, moving carefully over the curbs.

Later that night I tried to explain some of what I had heard to Freddy.

"The world is magic," I told him. "Can you feel it?"

We were lying in the grass in each other's arms. Over our heads, one of those yellow lights that attract insects was luring moths to destruction. I could hear them, even though I wasn't looking; hear their wings smacking against the bulb, the futile struggle of soft, many-colored bodies. Inside my eyes I saw them, a kaleidoscope that whirled without stopping.

But Freddy was beyond hearing. "You're magic," he said. "You're a witch." He pushed himself against my thighs. "Let me. Please."

But I couldn't let him. There were too many warnings, too many intrusions; walls I couldn't let down and he couldn't get over.

"You don't love me," he said.

My voice came out small, like a silver flute. "I love you too much."

For that time, it was enough.

The day before I left for vacation, I told the professor how the garden was like a rose, how we stepped into the perfumed heart that folded around us like petals.

"I don't want to go on vacation," I said. "I don't want to leave."

"Of course not." He was staring down the street as if something far away had captured his attention and he was listening to it, but his face was sad. "No one wants to be expelled from Paradise, but we are anyway."

I thought that was a horrible thing to say, dooming me to a life of wandering, and I said so.

He smiled that off-center smile of his. "We're all wanderers until we find there's no reason to be. That there's nothing out there so important. Just be sure and come back, will you?"

"Of course I'm coming back," I said, cross. "Where else would I go?"

"Write me a letter," he said. "Tell me what the ocean is like."

"Haven't you been there?"

"A long time ago. I'd like to know it again. I'd like you to see it for me. You can read the letter when you come back."

The idea felt like bribery, but I didn't say so. "Alright," I said.

That evening Freddy held me and cried. "Stay with me. Stay all night. Don't go. Let me love you."

Though I couldn't explain it to him I was, despite my womanly breasts, my open arms, as much a child as he was. And I held him like one holds a child. "I'll be back," I said. "It's only two weeks. Wait for me."

"I will," he promised. "I will."

We wrote. I lay on the sand composing letters, reading the post cards he sent. I never once looked at the sea or knelt over the tidal pools and their jewels as I had always done, except once when I found a star fish dead, drifting, a stillborn leaf. On my knees, I wept.

All I sent to the Professor was a post card with a short message about sea gulls and salt, quickly written and forgotten, a duty note like those sent to elderly relatives which, in a way, was how I thought of him when I thought of him at all.

When I got home I went straight to Isabel's. She admired my tan at great length.

"What's the matter?" I asked. "What's happened?"

"Nothing. Really." She turned away to look for her cigarettes.

"What's that mean?" I could hear my voice rising. The Professor would cringe.

"I took Tina to a party," she said, blowing a cloud of smoke. "She thought Freddy was cute."

"They all do."

"Well, he kind of liked her, too, but nothing happened."

I looked at her sitting there, her hands between her knees, unable to believe that a friend would do a thing like that. "Why did you have to take her there anyway?" I asked.

"She was here. We didn't have anything else to do. I didn't mean anything. I didn't think."

"You never do. That's your trouble." I knew I sounded nasty. I knew I was afraid.

It rained that night, one of those August rains that are precursors of fall, when the air smells of old leaves, damp, and ripening grapes, when the intangible scent of roses has gone.

Tina was small and thin, a sparrow next to me, and she had little, moving fingers that clasped and unclasped as she spoke. I hated her, more as a type than as rival, but certainly as that.

She also had mouse-brown hair that, newly cut, hugged her head like a cap making her boyish and oddly appealing.

"Where'd you leave your hair?" Fred asked her.

And she replied, her fingers twining like vines, her eyes gleaming with mischief, "On some man's pillow."

With that answer, I knew my fate. I had lost because of some notion of sin or fear, and because, in my innocence, I was unable to cope.

Love is negotiable. We barter for it, or we do not, and perhaps we are always the loser. Who can say? I couldn't. Not that night. That night I drank. And I watched them, Freddy and Tina, circling one another, laughing, finally disappearing into the garden, the night.

I drank more, and ended up in a car with Jeff Wills, thinking I'd show them all how little I cared. But Jeff was a gentleman. He let me cry on his shoulder while the rain fell. Then he returned me to the party.

Freddy drove me home, Tina's tiny bones between us, and the windshield wipers going shush . . . shush . . . like a heart.

"Take care of yourself," he said as I got out of the car and felt my way through rain and darkness to the door.

"You, too," I said, bending my head to the lock and unable to find it. "You, too. Take care."

I lay in bed for two days crying.

"You're crying over that dumb boy," my mother said. "I wish you'd stop. I told you, didn't I?"

Expelled from Paradise, I curled into myself and wept.

"Liza, Liza," the Professor said when my voice cracked and I sat there sorrowing. "Don't grieve. You're young. You have a whole life ahead of you. You'll get over it. You will. Believe me."

I couldn't tell him that my life was already over. How tell a blind man that? Even one who reached out with seeking fingers to touch my face with a gentleness that nearly broke my heart.

"Don't," I said. "Please. Don't."

He withdrew his hand and resumed his seat. Then, cocking his head at its precise angle said, "Page one hundred and fifty-nine. That's where we stopped."

"I remember," I said.

What I remembered later, too late to make reparation, was how his face, from that moment on, took on the lines, the shadows of the mask of tragedy; how his mouth turned down in the universal gesture of despair; and how he never spoke to me again of anything that touched the heart.

THE POPPY FIELD

THERE WERE four of us in Bologna that summer—Bologna La Grassa, The Fat—as it is called by those who know its pleasures. Paul and I were on our honeymoon; Christian Devries, who had been Paul's teacher, and his wife Flora, went every summer. They stayed in a pensione for three dollars a night, saving enough to indulge their delight in Bolognese cuisine and to embellish their wardrobes and their house with purchases of handmade clothing and seventeenth-century paintings and antiquities.

No one in the city believed that Christian and Flora were married. The rumor went that his real wife was a hopeless invalid whom he left at home for three months of the year while he sported with Flora, his mistress. A natural assumption to the romantic and tryst-loving Italians, for both Christian and Flora were startlingly flamboyant.

Winter or summer, Flora wore no underwear, a fact made apparent to the discerning Italian eye by her tremendous and unfettered breasts that thrust and jiggled as she walked. And what a walk! Her rear swished in concert with her front, while her tiny feet in three-inch heels tripped and clattered along the arcaded sidewalks, and her long, dark, and unbound hair tossed behind her like the mane of a mare.

Christian was short, bald, and round like the statue of the dwarf in the Boboli Gardens, and he wore white, hand-tailored linen suits and carried a walking stick, the handle of which was a bust of Venus carved out of gold. Neither before nor since had Bologna, that city of noble eccentrics, seen their like.

Looking back it seems that we were, all of us, actors playing our parts, and that I was the only one confused by the unreality. I had no desire to play a role, yet, surrounded by worldly and exotic people, was forced into one that was alien, that I wore with discomfort, feeling foolish and separate both from my companions and from Italy, the land of my ancestors.

Looking back I can see that Paul, though he spoke to me of love, was in love with a dream that was not me, and that it was there, in Bologna, that he began to fashion me the way a sculptor fashions clay, into a creature resembling his ideal, into a miniature copy of Flora.

This was not against my will because I was unconscious of his intentions, but against my nature, that of the true Italian as opposed to the mimic; that of the sensuous not of the sensual; of the optimist with face held to the sun, much as my grandmother had been. She who, at the end of a bleak Maine winter would run out, arms wide, shouting, "Il sole! Il sole!"

I carried a knowledge of Italy in my blood, my childhood memories. Christian, Flora, Paul, though they spoke the language fluently, though they aped the customs, the gestures, the culture, were impostors, foreigners unhappy with themselves, and they took my silence, born of timidity, for approval of their game.

Our days had a pattern. In the mornings, Christian, who was an art historian, a connoisseur, and a passionate collector, wrote those long, learned treatises on the art of the Renaissance and Baroque periods for which he was famous, and Flora typed his output, scrawled with a quill pen and India ink, on the portable typewriter that went with them everywhere.

Paul and I would have breakfast at the Central Bar; a pastry, freshly squeezed blood orange juice, cafe latté foaming with hot milk. And then my education would begin.

We went to museums, galleries, churches, antique shops. To the goldsmith's where we were having a necklace made, one much like Flora's that had been copied from a Holbein painting. To the dressmaker's, a spinster the size of a mouse, known to us as The Ghermanda. The Ghermanda had been discovered by Flora who kept her busy most of the summer sewing those form-fitting garments, each with the decolletage wherein quivered her much-admired breasts.

As a friend of Flora's, I was immediately taken on as client. Compared to hers, my needs were simple. Two dresses from the bright scarlet and blue linen we had purchased from the mills in Lyons. Paul wanted them low-cut a la Flora. The Ghermanda tsk-tsked around a mouthful of pins. Although wizened and subservient, she possessed the faultless Italian sense of style.

"No, no, Signore. Questa Signora qui non é la Signora Flora."

That was true enough. I was not Flora. The Ghermanda and I looked at one another in instant and complete agreement. But she was clever, that tiny woman with fingers like dry twigs that pinned, fit, measured. She gave Paul the decolletage—in the back—in as subtle a demonstration of one-upmanship as I have seen. I had, she informed me in the privacy of her fitting room, where no gentlemen were permitted, *ever*, "Una bella figura." Perfect for clothes. Not too much like some, eh?—a gesture describing Flora—and not too little.

She was a perfectionist. The fittings went on for ten days while Paul paced the marble floor of the waiting room fearing an atrocity for which he would be forced to pay.

On the eleventh day, she slipped one of the dresses over my

head and busied herself with hooks and snaps. Finally she stepped back and gestured at me to view myself in her triple mirror.

"Ecco," she said proudly around the ever-present pins.

I looked at myself once, twice, three times. I twirled. In the back the dress began at my waist. In front a series of invisible tucks and darts provided support, emphasized my breasts. The skirt spilled out around me like petals. I giggled.

"Perfetto, no?" she asked, eyes sly behind her spectacles.

"Assolutamente," I assured her.

"Do *you* like it?" Paul asked, staring with bewilderment at the modish me. He had not yet made up his mind whether he wanted me to look like a mistress and behave like a nun, or the reverse.

"Yes," I said. "It's wild."

"I guess. I just hope it isn't too wild." He fumbled for his wallet, then took the Ghermanda aside and argued in a low voice over the price, embarrassing me. The woman was poor, existing in two rooms of a subdivided seventeenth-century palazzo, cooking her simple meals on a hot plate and sleeping on a cot behind the fitting room.

"Don't bargain," I said. "Just pay her."

He shook his head. "Let me handle this. It's what you do. They expect it."

I didn't think so. You pay for artistry. Gladly. In the fitting room I pinned what *lire* I had to the curtain and came out hastily lest it be discovered.

From the Ghermanda's we would go to one of the hundred churches, to the museums, to the famous Due Torri, the Two Towers, and always Paul lectured me on the history, the aesthetics of what we were seeing. Why Francia was a better artist than Michelangelo; why the brothers Caracci were the best—yet currently the most unpopular—artists of the period. Berenson's fault, of course. He had labeled them "eclectic," when, if the truth were known, they were superbly Bolognese, products of the most sensual city in the world.

Around noon Christian and Flora would find us, and Christian would add his statements to Paul's, taking over the lecture, contributing to what he called, *"L'educazione di Giovanna,"* as if I were the subject of a novel or a kind of social experiment.

I let their words deluge me without revealing my hunger for silence. My approach to art, perhaps naive, was then and now intuitive. I look at, I enter a painting. I taste, touch, absorb it. It gives to me. If it does not, I move on to the next. It is the same with churches, towns, monuments, streets. If we cannot partake of one another, I go on.

The same, I suppose, could be said of Paul and me, except that I did not, could not move on when I realized that what we had labeled "love" was something other, an intellectual meeting that left the physical, the sensual untouched. What we had ultimately was a sense of barter, of the giving and taking of actions. He educated me, bought me food, dresses, jewels; I acquiesced to his wants. Our bargain had been struck.

It was Flora who enlightened me. We were sitting in an outdoor cafe discussing where we would go for dinner in that city of restaurants, trattorias, cafes, where meals could be had—then—for two dollars, and where the act, the *art* of eating was the second most popular topic, the art of sex being first.

"Augusto gives free drinks as a reward for eating a lot," Flora said.

"But Diana has *porcini* this week," I countered. I was having a love affair with those large, grilled mushrooms that tasted like meat.

Christian raised his eyebrows. "Ladies," he pronounced, bowing toward each of us in turn, "you have such exquisite and expensive taste." His tone was simultaneously damning and praising, as if our value as objects was increased by our demands.

"Then let's go to Gino's on the cheap," I said. "I don't care."

Paul frowned at me. Christian was not to be treated as a mere mortal. He was the elder statesman to be idolized, imitated, revered. I felt trapped between them.

Christian tapped his glass of *Punt e Mes*. "We will go," he said, savoring his words and the image behind them, "we will go to

San Pietro in Casals. Giovanna must try the *ucellini* baked in a loaf."

I did not share the Italian passion for little birds—starlings, pigeons, doves, whatever was shot or raised. I preferred my birds singing, on the wing.

"Now, now, Giovanna," he said, reading my expression, "you have to try it."

"Alright," I said. And to Flora, "What will you wear?"

She shrugged and sipped her aperitif. "Something outlandish," she said. "As usual."

"What?" I said.

"You heard me. Something that everybody will laugh at the way they always do."

I cringed away from the acid in her voice. "Then why do you? Nobody makes you?"

She looked across the little table at the two men who were deep in the analysis of two sculptured angels we had seen earlier. "It makes Christian happy," she said in a low voice. "It makes him feel good to possess what everyone desires so I do it. That's all."

"But, Flora. That's impossible. You have a say in how you look."

"Do I?"

"You should."

She shrugged again, that voluptuous movement that set her bosom to nearly overflowing its bounds. "I have a good life," she said. "I pay for it."

"But . . ." I said.

She rose, chin in the air. "I'm late for my ballet lesson. Wear what you like. Christian?"

"Yes, yes, my love," he said, rising to accompany her to what was not a lesson as much as an exercise session to keep her curves under strict muscular control.

I wondered if this, too, wasn't Christian's idea, worshipper of the classic ideal that he was, and if Flora would have preferred to be shaped by artifice rather than will power.

"We'll meet beside the fountain at five," he said.

I watched them make their way across the plaza, past the Fountain of Neptune, the subject of which seemed to be pointing at them as they passed.

"You know he makes her dress like that," I said to Paul. "She just told me."

He emptied his glass. "You misunderstood. He doesn't *make* her do anything. He knows what's right for her. That's all."

"How can it be right if she feels ridiculous?" I asked, fighting not so much for Flora as for my own individuality.

He shook his head. "She doesn't. I think that's obvious."

To persist was useless. Besides, it had been Paul who had arranged for my own lessons, in Gino's Restaurant when it closed for the afternoon. I was learning to cook like a Bolognese, like Flora—*ragu, tortellini, scallopi di vitello.*

"I'm late, too," I said. "I'll just run over to Gino's. Take your time."

"I'll come with you," he said as he always did, as if he were afraid that on my own I'd come to some conclusion about myself. He had never, however, come with me into the kitchen. "Women's stuff," he called it, laughing. He went up to our hotel room and took siesta with the shutters closed against the heat and casting strips of shadow across the bed.

And I? I reveled in freedom. In the familiarity of being with women who had no artifice; who chattered, gossiped, laughed, chopped, rolled out dough that became pasta, who orchestrated the movements of the kitchen as a choreographer does ballet, and who were eager to know the truth about Christian and Flora from me, the insider.

Were they married? Truly? Ahhh! Such a pair! And how devoted he was. As if she were made of glass. They rolled their eyes and minced around the worktable in imitation. They clapped their hands at the sight of my new necklace, at the lapis earrings dangling from tiny strands of pearls. How lucky I was! My husband, too, adored me. Here was the proof. Men were such odd creatures, you never knew. But then, I was on my honeymoon. The *luna di mella.* All was romance. Ah, yes!

And while we talked, while our fingers flew over chicken livers, garlic, parsley, onions, the light would come through the window, that golden and dazzling light intensified by white walls that is peculiar to Italy, and I would remember my grandmother's kitchen, the clouds of flour hovering in the air as she mixed and rolled her dough, her orange cat perched in the sunlight next to the pot of geraniums. I had been at home there, and was in this place, too, with these earthy women and their talk of love. I belonged among the copper pots and rolling pins far more than in concert halls or the shops of obsequious goldsmiths. Inside, I sighed. What had I, creature of the senses, done?

Wednesday was market day; the noisy day of festivity and sales that turned the baroque bricks of the piazza into chaos. And Gino's wife, Yolande, my teacher, had decided that I, her pupil, needed to learn ingredients from the farmer's stall to the final disguise on the plate. Besides, she was lonely. Her daughter had married an engineer from Abruzzi and never came home. Never. Such ingratitude!

So on Wednesdays I woke early, shortly after the bar in the alley between the hotel and the cathedral had lost its last, shouting patron. I woke to the smell and rattle of motorcycles and farm trucks, to the clopping of the hooves of donkeys, the expletives of drivers. I dressed in the dark, quickly, lest Paul hear me, waken, and call me back, and I slipped out the door and into the street where Yolande waited, baskets on each arm.

"Andiamo, andiamo!" she would greet me. "Oggi ch'e lamponi, fresca, fresca!" Mouth-watering raspberries to be served floating in fresh cream.

Together we sampled them, poked the plumpness of chickens and ducks, measured the crispness of lettuces, and hefted tomatoes, eyed the fat in Parma hams and thumped the yellow globes of cheeses. We examined the flesh and the eyes of fish, and hoped the fringed mussels on their beds of seaweed were uncontaminated for the pasta alla marinara that was served on Fridays to the devout.

The purchase of wine was left to Gino who scoured the countryside at harvest time and returned with great wicker-covered jugs that he stored in the basement and sometimes in the bathtub and dispensed in flagons at the table.

Between the stalls I would be pinched by the old farmers, men in ill-fitting black suits and porkpie hats who mistook me for a native. Always, I laughed and nodded, accepting their attention as a compliment, for as such was it intended.

"The old devil," Yolande would snort. "And you young enough to be his daughter. Men never change. They reach out from their coffins."

The pattern was as old as Penelope's tapestry—men, women love, death, intrigue. I understood it far better than I understood the intellect, that peculiar labyrinth that makes sense of emotion, that regulates instinct with reason.

And when I left Yolande and went back to the room, bearing at the very least a streak of crimson juice on my chin, and often a pot of geraniums or, as summer deepened, chrysanthemums in shades of bronze and yellow, I would find Paul still asleep and would sit by the open window smoking and changing back into a wife. Sometimes, however, he would be soaking in the huge tub, and he would say, "You have juice on your chin," and reach out to kiss me.

I would evade his arms, unable to make the change from earth to air, and feel stricken at my own dishonesty. And then, angry, he would tell me to wash my face, to straighten myself, that I should not be seen in the streets like a peasant for then what would people think of him? And I would scrub and try to placate him with a smile.

That afternoon, however, I chopped garlic and clams and tried to tell Yolande what Flora had said. She listened, straining over my inadequacies with the language, her mouth open in sympathy.

"Poverina," she said. Then her face brightened. The professore, she said, was old. Perhaps he would die leaving her with those jewels, those breasts, like la Loren, and then she could find herself a young lover. Perhaps it was better so.

Flora, I thought, would have died at having her life explained, plotted out by a mere cook, but I laughed and agreed. And I took my time returning to the hotel, making a detour to the street of the lace-makers where I lingered, looking in shop windows until the striking of the clock in the campanile startled me.

I hardly had time to dress, to slip on the Ghermanda's scarlet creation and hang my new gold chain around my neck.

Paul paced in front of the shuttered window. "Hurry," he urged. "We shouldn't keep Christian waiting."

"Who does he think he is?" I asked. "The Principe de Herculeno?" that mythical figure with which mothers frightened their disobedient children.

He turned on his heel. "You've changed," he said. "You're not you anymore."

"Have I?"

"Yes," he said, "and it's not very nice. You act mad all the time."

"I'm sorry," I said. "I didn't notice."

He set his chin, and his lower lip protruded like a child's. "Maybe you should," he said. "Now let's go." He held open the door and I went through, my skirt flaring around my thighs.

"Clever," said Flora when she saw the dress. "Very nice." She was wearing grey silk wrapped tightly, and two golden arm bracelets in the shape of serpents.

I twirled in response.

"What a lovely back you have, Giovanna," Christian said, coming close and peering at me. "Lovely, indeed. An odalisque. French, I think."

I smiled at him and got into the car. He got in beside me after seating Flora and Paul side by side in the back, and gave me directions, now and then casting me a look of approval.

It was a golden evening, reminiscent of a thousand landscape paintings. Olive and poplar trees lifted their leaves in the late sunlight, and the fields of ripening hay were spattered with poppies that fluttered and swayed and nodded their crimson heads as we passed.

The restaurant sat at the edge of a field. Tables were set on the terrace, and as we sat, drinking aperitifs and talking idly, the scent of grass, the color of the poppies swept over me with an unendurable sweetness. I wanted to touch them; to gather them; I wanted the whole earth and radiant sky in my arms.

I got up and leaned on the balustrade. Behind me voices faded away, and I heard the wind, the swish of grasses. And then I was running through the field startling a flock of small birds that rose whistling into the air and whirled above my head while I pulled at the tough stems and thrust my face into the hearts of the blossoms.

When I had made a bouquet—grasses, seed-heads, superlative poppies—I made my way back to the three who were staring at me open-mouthed. Paul and Flora were frowning. Christian was smiling widely and clapping his hands.

"Brava, Giovanna," he called. "Every landscape needs a figure to make it memorable. Una bella figura." He lifted his glass high in a toast.

I deposited the bouquet in Flora's lap, and then she, too, began to smile, passing flowers around the table like a beneficent goddess overflowing with grace.

Paul's frown vanished. "To Giovanna," he said.

"To Giovanna," they echoed.

Shortly after that, Paul and I went on to Rome. He never mentioned the incident, and after awhile it seemed forgotten.

When we arrived back in the States, I was pregnant, and then pregnant again, and any thoughts that I had had about individuality, about a possible career of my own, were submerged in motherhood and compromise. I never went back to Italy. I hardly thought of it except as a series of struggles touched by moments of light.

The Ghermanda's dresses hung in the closet, scarlet and blue and too small for the me I became, and one day I packed them, not without regret, into a box to be given to the poor.

"How can you do that? Just throw them away?" Paul demanded, as if they were tangible proof of former happiness, talismans to be kept in a trunk between sheets of tissue paper and bags of lavender.

"They're only clothes," I said, but I was disturbed by his hurt as I always was. It seemed to signify a lack in me, an inability to complete an expected happiness, to recall my own history with the devotion he believed it deserved.

But what of that history? As far as I knew I had done nothing memorable. I had married, borne children, kept house; been a silent partner attending dutifully to the stability of the world. If anything were to be stored in a trunk, it should have been my dreams, my failures, my placidity in the face of it all.

I left the dresses in the box and delivered them along with the children's outgrown sweaters and snowsuits to the parish church. Then, reluctant to return home in the splendor of the October afternoon, I threaded my way across town to the suburbs where Christian and Flora lived surrounded by a lifetime's treasures.

Over the years we had become friends, and they welcomed my visits that I made to assure myself that they weren't lonely or in need, for there were only the two of them, grown old despite Yolande's prediction. Christian used his walking stick out of necessity, and Flora seemed to have grown smaller and wore ruffles to her chin. Yet around them still hovered that air of elegance, the imminence of a grand gesture, like retired actors still able to summon strength for a role.

"Do you remember," Christian said as we sat on the terrace, "do you remember how once we were all young, and you were the youngest of all? Do you remember the evening you danced in the poppy field in a dress the color of flowers?"

I hadn't thought of it in years, but I nodded.

"You were so alive. So young. I quite loved you. Did you know?"

I shook my head.

"Ah well," he said, "it was long ago. But it could have been yesterday. Beauty is timeless. I've believed that all my life." He cocked his head, ostensibly listening to Flora's approach, but perhaps to hide what looked like tears in his eyes.

As she entered carrying a tray with a decanter and glasses, he struggled to his feet. "Let me help you, my dear," he said, as courtly as he had always been.

She eluded him with a flourish, setting the tray on a polished table and watching as he poured amber sherry.

"Not too much. Doctor's orders," she reminded him.

"Nonsense. I wish to make a toast. What does a doctor know about it?"

He raised his glass to us. "To beauty," he said simply.

And as I raised my glass to his, memory played a trick, or the sunlight did. We were back, all of us, at the edge of a field, and it seemed that nothing had touched us; not age, or illness, or years of making compromises to secure ourselves. We were like the poppies lifting year after year into bloom. In the midst of them I was dancing in a scarlet dress the color of petals, and at the edge Flora sat laughing and tossing her hair, flinging abundance everywhere.

PART II

THE AGE OF INSECTS

THE AGE OF INSECTS

THEY WERE HAVING breakfast in the motel coffee shop; Rosemary and Howard, Howard's mother and the baby, Rick, who was crumbling saltines on the tray of his chair. The floor beneath was littered with crumbs and plastic wrappers.

"Now you *stop!*" Howard's mother said to him, giving his wrist a little slap.

To Rosemary she said, "You shouldn't let him make such a mess. What'll the waitress think?"

Rosemary shrugged and sipped her coffee. "He's a baby," she said. "And he's cutting a tooth. Leave him be."

"I never had that trouble with Howard," his mother said. "He never made messes. And he was toilet trained by this age, too."

"Wonderful," said Howard. He buttered a piece of toast and cut it neatly in half. "And now let's drop the subject if you don't mind."

Rosemary said, as she felt she had said a hundred times in the last week, "They learn when they're ready."

"Dat?" Rick said suddenly, pointing to the window, beyond which a strip of beach and ocean shimmered. "Dat?"

"What-is-that?" Howard's mother leaned across the table. "Say, what-is that?"

"Dat?" Rick said. "Dat? Dat? Dat?"

Rosemary followed the direction of his finger. On the beach teen-agers in bikinis, men in bright shorts, women in beach robes hauling toddlers were hurrying toward the inlet. They were all pointing, waving their arms, shouting, although the shouting was muted by the distance and the glass.

Rick pushed himself up in his chair and kicked his heels, and Rosemary took advantage of his action. She scooped him out, set him on his feet. "You two finish," she said. "Rick and I will go see what's happening."

"Be careful," Howard said. "Come back as soon as you know what's going on."

"You shouldn't give in to him so easily. Make him finish his juice," Howard's mother said, picking up the sticky glass and waving it at Rick. "Juicy. Come drink."

Rosemary set her chin as Rick buried his face in her neck. "We'll go see," she said to him. She buckled him into his stroller, backed it through the door, and then, nearly running, wheeled down the sandy path toward the beach.

"Free at last," she said to the top of his brown head. "You hear?"

"Dat?" He twisted around to look up at her with round blue eyes.

"Old Busy Body," she said. "Say that one. Go ahead. Say Old Busy Body."

He grinned at her and waved his arms in the air as if to urge her on. "Hoozy buzzy," he said. "Buzzy, buzzy."

For a moment she wanted to gallop, to abandon him and the stroller, the ties that bound her to family, to earth, to talk. She wanted to run into the wind, alone and deaf to the whine of instructions.

She caught up with a woman in a red and yellow beach coat and sunglasses. "What's going on?" she asked.

The woman had black hair in pink plastic rollers and looked, with her dark glasses, her flowered coat, like an exotic species of grasshopper. "Whale on the beach," she said. "Must've come in last night on the high tide."

"Is it alive?"

The woman shrugged, the flowers rising and falling as if the earth trembled. "Don't know," she said. "I've never seen one close up, though. Have you?"

"No. Just some swimming last week. They were pretty big."

They had been driving down the coast on their way here and suddenly there the whales were, big as boats or hillsides, moving leisurely, effortlessly southward, secure in their strength, their size.

She had stopped the car and run to the edge of the cliff and stood staring after them wishing . . . she wasn't sure what she had wished except that the ocean seemed empty when they had gone, and she felt empty, too, lacking in grace, hungry for giants.

Back in the car she drove faster than usual, racing them, trying to catch up. How did it feel, she wondered, to be all of a piece and rippling, to be one long muscle?

She was imagining it, rolling in the waves in her mind, when Howard's mother had said, "You never stop. I need to stop. You never think about me."

So Rosemary pulled in at a gas station, stayed with the car by the pumps, the dry air hot, alien, the sun on the concrete burning her eyes. Were all people so intrusive, or was it only this woman who was, now, a part of her family?

She didn't know, didn't really want to know, to dig into the necessities of relationships. If she did she might be forced into action, might cut herself off from what was safe, familiar, predictable, and be caught, helpless, in the great current of her own desires.

She got a Coke from the machine just as Howard's mother emerged, beaming, from the rest room. "This big boy used the toilet," she said. "Isn't that fine?"

"I wish you'd stop. I really wish you would. You'll just make him nervous."

Her mother-in-law waved her hand in a gesture of dismissal. "You should thank me. Think about no diapers."

"I'd rather have a happy kid." Rosemary threw the can into the trash and headed for the car in the hope of ending the conversation.

"Life isn't happy. You should know that by now. And you drink too much of that stuff." The words buzzed after her, shattering the air.

"It has its moments," she said. In her head she turned whale again, diving deep, the only sounds those of water and the thin music of the others, ahead, around.

Now on the beach a chartreuse Volkswagen with oversized tires and filled with gesticulating teen-agers roared past. It, too, looked like a grotesque insect, myriad legs waving.

The whole world is filled with bugs, she thought. Beetles, grasshoppers, locusts, mosquitoes that hover and bite and make you itch.

She remembered reading somewhere that we live in the age of insects, outnumbered, threatened by extinction from their devouring jaws. The age of behemoths was over except for the shy whales gliding at the base of land, circling it in secrecy and silence.

She pushed the stroller faster over the hard sand. Now she could see the small bay, the islands clustered in oriental delicacy at its mouth, see the shifting and multicolored wave of people that danced around something grey and huge and still, and in that stillness menacing, as if it were gathering itself for assault, for a last rearing, a final smash of tail that would gouge the beach, bury the swarm of minutiae at its flanks.

"My God," said the insect woman coming alongside her. "Isn't that something? Isn't that really the end?"

Rick kicked the backstop of his stroller and leaned forward. "Uh, uh, uh," he said, meaning, "Go!"

"Yes, baby. In a minute." She had the feeling that she needed to approach with dignity, with caution. What if it moved? Sang? She didn't think she could bear to hear it calling for home, for its mate.

It had, perhaps, gotten lost in the fog, become disoriented by the current, always strong at the inlet. And there had been a fog last night. She remembered hearing the horn, insistent, muffled. She remembered Howard swimming beside her, equally insistent, and her own cry, like an echo from the sea quickly stilled, lest the old woman, wrapped in sleep, hear and come forth clattering and shrill.

She remembered she had stood afterwards at the window looking out into the fog until Howard came and whispered, "Come back. There's a draft. You'll get cold." But she hadn't been cold. Not at all. She had opened the window and lapped the fog like a beast.

"What's the matter?" he asked, and she said, "Nothing." And nothing was the matter, really, except she needed to be out there naked, the grey mist touching her, and the waves, the little, foam-topped splashings, creeping around her feet.

Had the whale even then been moving up the channel, the great, blunt head steering between islands, feeling the way? Had its sonar malfunctioned, or had it been trapped, lacking room to turn and flee back to the deep? Or had it been lured by the voice of the foghorn, a siren, and the beast helpless in the song, the desire?

Well, it was here now, dead or dying, and all the inhabitants of the peninsula, winged and otherwise, had turned out for the wake.

A pickup and a convertible had joined the Volkswagen and were racing on the sand, using the length of the carcass as a marker. The roar of the engines was nerve-wracking, even at a distance, and Rosemary debated about turning back.

The residents of the trailer camp over the hill were coming now; kids on tricycles, women in shorts and halters carrying coffee cups, and everywhere adolescents with radios blaring, the music, the rhythms clashing. They came in a streaming line, an army of fire ants, a great platoon of dancing wasps to feast upon the fallen.

Helpless, she was caught up, swept along, while Rick pounded the stroller and let out yelps of excitement that grew more frequent as they drew closer to the whale.

She could smell it now, oily, and salty, too, like seaweed decomposing in the sun, like the sea bottom, flesh, plant, and brine and not unpleasant, just alien in the air, on the earth.

"What a stink!" The grasshopper, still at her side, had her lips drawn back from her teeth. "They'd better get it out of here quick."

"How?" Rosemary asked. "How are they going to move that?"

The woman shrugged, disturbing the flowers once more. "I sure don't know. Helicopters maybe. Dynamite. They got ways." She looked down at Rick. "Cute kid," she said. "Look at the fishie. Big, big fishie."

"Dat?" said Rick.

"Whale," Rosemary said. "Whale."

They were nearing the tail, the great flukes spread like wings or a propeller gone askew. Where it joined the body, some early comer had hacked out rude initials in the grey flesh. JB and MA. Flies clustered over the wound. There were old scars, too, battle scars, run-ins with the screws of ships. Who knew, now? It had survived those things, drawn to a different dying.

Rosemary put out her hand and touched it.

"Yuk!" the woman said. "How can you do that? What's it feel like?"

"Kind of like a tire," Rosemary said. "Hard. Cool." She shivered. Alive, was it warm, mammalian, soft? She didn't know, and no one here could tell her or even cared.

They were pelting it with fists of gravel and soft drink cans, kicking at it with sneakered feet, stabbing the barnacled hide with penknives, stones, anything that came to hand, their laughter merging with the cacophony of radios, the buzzing of flies, the roar of engines.

Near the great head one eye stared, lightless, through a film of gnats, and two boys stood urinating happily against the slack jaw.

At that moment Rosemary moved, the wall of protection she had erected around herself broken. She heard herself shouting above the primal chorus as she moved toward the two. "Stop it! Stop it right now!"

They turned their heads, grinning foolishly, their water cut off in surprise.

"It's dead, ain't it?" The older of the two recovered first and stared at her.

"Didn't you ever learn respect for things? For animals? For the dead? Didn't you?"

He stuffed himself back into his shorts. "It's only a fish, lady," he said. "A big, stinking fish. Where'd you come from? Outer space?"

"It's a mammal," she said. "It was alive once like you and me. It *was* like you and me." But as she spoke she felt more kinship with the whale than with these two defiant specimens.

"Yeah, yeah," the second said. "A mammal. Come on, let's split this scene. It stinks." He gave her a mock salute, dribbled a final offering at her feet.

She ran at them then, her fists doubled. "Little pigs!" she yelled. "Blood suckers! Get out! Get out!"

They went into a backwards run, arms and legs churning, faces contorted with laughter. "Pigs!" they chanted. "The lady says pigs, pigs, pig suckers!"

She turned and fled, bumping the stroller into holes in the sand, into bodies, running through piles of weed that caught on the wheels and streamed behind like tattered rags.

At the narrow entrance to the path she looked back at the mass of bodies rising, falling, dancing around the corpse. For a moment she felt that she was floating above the world, so high that all history seemed to happen at once; an eruption of seas and volcanos, amoebas and wings, fins and the hesitant groping of fingers around others, around torn and smoking air.

"Uh, uh, uh." Rick's voice rose shrill as his father and grandmother came toward them.

"Are you alright? What took you so long? What's going on

down there?" Howard's hair, the same brown as Rick's, fell over his forehead.

"A whale," she said. She lurched toward the shade of his body blindly. "Don't go. Stay here. Please let's. It's dead."

His mother craned her neck, squinted past them small-eyed in the sun. "I want to go," she said. "I want to go see the whale."

And before Rosemary could stop her she was going down the path, moving jerkily in the manner of the old, elbows flashing, pale, shapeless legs and crooked feet feeling a tentative way over the glaring sand and into the debris of the last high tide.

THE LOVER OF SWAMPS

I SUMMER

MINNA'S HUSBAND AND MINE are naturalists. All summer long they rise at sunup to count birds, tie radio transmitters around the necks of turtles, or run through pastures holding recording equipment on the ends of poles.

Minna and I keep haphazard house, take nature walks with our children learning the names of flowers out of the guidebook, and spend hours on the small beach outside our cabins.

And I write. I am always writing, feeling my way through a morass of words toward something. I write, and then I rush to read it to Minna or to watch her read it herself, her blue eyes narrowed in concentration.

Minna is my best friend. She is joyous, intelligent, and kind. She nurtures me, which is what I need at this point in my life. She listens when I talk, understands the gropings of my poems. And she is never shocked, even when I tell her that the man I love kissed me passionately in my kitchen.

She laughs as if it is exciting, which of course it is, the more so because removed from it, we may analyze and ponder.

"You need to love," she says. "That's how you are. Don't worry about it. Just enjoy."

Of course I need to love, and I don't worry. The situation is romantic and gives me a focal point for my feelings that are those of adolescence, unmanageable and tumultuous. I can't imagine writing poetry to Peter, for example. I'm married to him. Besides, he is more interested in the body count of midges than in my emotions. Does the mosquito feel? Does the mayfly know passion in its one-night stand? Personally, I don't discount the possibility. Life hums with the excitement of survival. Peter, has never questioned the existence of invertebrate feelings, nor, to be truthful, is he very much interested in mine. "Women's stuff," he said of one of my poems. After that, I never showed him another.

In contrast, I can send the man I love all of my work, and he will write or phone and tell me, "Keep on! Keep on!" He plays the violin and travels a lot, and thus we have an artistic and chaste affair with desire kept under wraps except after concerts and once a year in the confines of my house where we kiss, and very deftly, part.

Now Minna giggles. "How did it happen? Did he just grab you or what?"

"I told him he inspired me. That his music made me want to do the same thing with words. Touch people. Make them feel. Make them see." This is true. I would like to be as magical with language as he is with music, but it is difficult when one is only finding the way as I am.

She stops laughing. "He'd understand that," she says. "He's a musician. Sensitive. In his body."

Her statement pleases me. I like to talk about the language of bodies. Undercurrents fascinate me. The things felt but not said. Emotions expressed by a touch of the hand, the quirk of an eyebrow.

"Do you think he knows I love him?" I ask.

"Certainly."

"Then why doesn't he say something?"

I am always waiting for him to do or say something more, to make a declaration of undying passion, which he, the gentleman, never does. I was raised to believe in female passivity, in the value of unrequited yearnings, which I have come to believe are more trouble than they're worth.

She raises delicate brows. "Why don't you?"

"Me?" I say. "Me?" For me to make an advance is out of the question. Besides, it seems unromantic, in league with midge body counts and the sex life of the praying mantis. My strategy, if I have one, is to wait for emotion to overcome us both, for a kind of synchrony I know is not impossible. I do it here all the time with water, sky, the flights of geese. I achieve a oneness with the environment, a happiness, and I know it must happen between people, too, even between men and women, even with the pieces of the self.

"The time isn't right," I tell her. "You know what I mean."

She smiles, like a plucked string. "Yes," she says. "I know."

She sounds mysterious, filled with a secret knowledge, knowledge I must labor for but which she possesses without effort. Sometimes I think Minna is a witch—a white one of course, the kind who brews medicinal herbs and love potions in the dark of the moon.

"Are you happy?" I ask her suddenly, curious about her shadowed aura.

She flashes me a curious look, hard and flat like the stones we skip out over the water to amuse the children. "Let's say I'm not content," she answers. "I'd rather die than be content." And the way she says it rings with certainty and with a bitterness like salt.

I, of course, am not content either, though I am afraid to admit it. I am thrashing in my chains seeking a way out of a life that is gradually stifling me, a release for the words dammed in my throat. I have also developed an affinity with the swamp that stretches for miles behind the lake and forest.

It is a place of tendrils, vines, fecundity, and death. Everything there struggles out of mud toward light. Trees pound the sky. Millions of frogs shriek, warble, twang in a frenzy of mating. Beneath acres of spatterdock, sluggish water oozes and moves, so slowly as to be unnoticeable, toward the lake; hidden by leaves and dark water, turtles lie waiting for the unsuspecting bodies of ducklings, and on the fertile banks pitcher plants unfold sticky webs, trap flies, and eat them. I spend hours there ingesting patterns and shapes, the infinite varieties and methods of survival.

Minna always volunteers to watch the children so that I can go off on my solitary searches. "You need time alone," she says.

"What about you? Don't you need it, too?"

She smiles, that shiver of blue splinters. "I manage. Don't worry."

So I don't worry, though perhaps I should. Sometimes I feel guilty about the time that she dispenses so freely, but I soon forget. The swamp lures. My greed is monumental. Like a howl.

II AUTUMN

Summer slips away. I find woodbine turning scarlet, the flames of goldenrod lighting the fields. Overhead the geese whirl in practice flights and shriek in exhilaration. Soon I will be back in the city, housebound, trapped by snow and the glossing-over of feelings. Inside myself, I tremble.

Minna and I are sitting on a log staring at the water. She is not content this afternoon but filled with restless energy like a boat that pulls at its moorings. The lines of her body are taut against sky; the shadow she casts is long.

I wait for her to speak. I never force Minna, only create the right atmosphere. This is my gift to her—the permission to think aloud, the turning of self into a hollow of silence.

"I'm pregnant," she says suddenly, not looking at me.

I'm astounded, then repelled. Like me, her children are nearly grown. Like me she is almost free of the necessity to guard and educate, nurture and provide. She was almost ready to move on to other challenges, to do something for herself. Now within her, a cluster of cells demands attention and will grow more voracious with the passing of time.

"Why? Do you want it?" My first words are the worst I could have chosen.

But she laughs. "Of course. It's kind of my last chance, so I'm taking it."

I don't see the importance of producing more babies. What is important to me is the shape of the self, its function as other than vessel. "I guess I'm not a good mother," I say, frustrated by my efforts to understand.

Minna never lets me criticize myself. It is a trait that I love. She looks at me with ferocity. "Yes you are," she says. "You're just different from me." She frowns, a small gesture that is gone before it takes hold. "Besides, you have something else you have to do."

"What?"

"Write. You have to write. We do what we do best, what we have to do."

"Anybody can have babies." It is cruel. It is also true.

She stands up carefully. "Time for dinner," she says.

I have hurt her, but I don't know how to apologize without betraying myself, cutting deeper into the wound I've made. I stand, too. "What are you having?"

Leftovers."

"Peter won't eat leftovers. The last time I tried that he yelled and screamed and went out for dinner."

She sticks out her chin. "You should serve them anyhow. If he's hungry, he'll eat. Like I said, you've got other things to do."

Peter wouldn't eat them, though. He thinks he deserves the best, even when camping out. But Minna and I don't discuss domestic stress. One of the pleasures of our friendship is that we can almost forget we have husbands. We act like girls, the world filled with promise and ideas. At least we did. Now our easy acceptance of our situation has changed.

As it turns out, I am awed by Minna's gestation. She is, after all, creating life; words seem trivial by comparison. I am reduced to the status of onlooker, worshipper of fertility. This is easy for me, the lover of swamps.

We talk about physical changes and names for the baby. We mumble past experiences and old wives' tales, and after a time it becomes my child as much as hers, my body that has become awkward. I have even forgotten my lover in my expectations, and see nothing odd in this state, do not recognize it for a kind of distorted hunger.

As the months pass, I am in a fever of excitement. Will it be boy or girl? Will it look like Minna or Martin? I want to know. I am tired of waiting. I am worse even than Minna who sleeps a lot and doesn't say much.

During the long months of cold and snow I drift through the house wishing it were summer and we were all back by the lake watching the water and the blue weaving of damsel flies, so like our thoughts, sporadic but purposeful.

IV SPRING

The baby is stubborn and late.

Peter, the boys and I leave for the lake.

Minna tells me, "Use my desk if you want to be alone and write. We'll be there soon. *Five* of us."

She has a small blue kneehole desk at the window of her cabin. Sitting at it I can see new grass, a stand of Mayapples, quiet lake water. In late spring the lake is often still, as if it is holding its breath, cupping the tadpoles, the emerging dragonflies, the fingerlings in its warm bowl. I sit here often, writing little, following spirals of thought.

Sometimes I disappear into the swamp for hours. Sometimes Peter follows me. He chatters and spears the silence so I must run ahead to preserve my solitude. He tries to make conversation by saying things like, "Look at that sunset!" He wants to gain access to that place where my feelings are born, but he can't, and I am afraid to let him. Neither of us knows how to open to the other. He doesn't know that the act of entering should be mutually unconscious. I never speak of this. It is a danger too threatening to imagine.

In Minna's absence I write letters to everyone—old friends, my parents, even my lover who is somewhere making music. They are long letters filled with description and musings, and I do not expect answers. What I expect is that they will be read and understood for what they are—a shout from the wilderness. I must find ears to hear me.

I write to Minna. I tell her about the sparrow's nest in the grass outside her door. There are four, naked, sinewy infants in the down-lined cup. When I pass, they lift their heads and open their beaks so wide I could drop stones into them. I don't do this, but I could. Something about their insistence annoys me.

I am writing to her when the telephone rings. It is Martin. Minna has had a girl named Caroline. They will all be here next week.

In my excitement I clean her cabin, dusting, sweeping, destroying spider webs and mouse haunts. I go out and gather flowers—wild geraniums and prickly hawthorne, the first violets—and stuff them into one of the old milk bottles we use for vases. Naturally they are past their prime before Minna comes, so I go out and replenish, loving the ritual, the choosing, the feel of wet leaves and petals, the scents of flowers and newly released soil in the air.

When the car pulls up, Minna's kids tumble out and run to the water, picking up their relationship with mine as if the hiatus of winter never happened. Martin opens Minna's door, and she hands him a white-wrapped bundle, then gets out herself. She takes the bundle back and offers it to me.

I stand stiffly, holding the blanket that in its thickness forms a cocoon that may or may not contain a human form. I look at the little face. She looks like a raisin, still wrinkled, dark-haired. I think of a thing to say. All my expectations have taken flight. I hand the bundle back to Minna with a smile.

"Welcome back," I say. "I missed you."

She is white-faced with a kind of wildness in her eyes. The smile she gives me in return is ghastly, the grimace of a skull. Something is wrong.

It does not take long to discover the problem. Minna is obsessed with Caroline. She does not put the bundle down but carries it everywhere, clutching it with ferocity. She is the primal mother, lacking only the lashing tail.

I am the only one who notices Minna's metamorphosis. Martin, the happy father, is calm and smiling. Peter, as usual, is unobservant. The men disappear talking happily about insect swarms. Minna, with absolute disregard, unbuttons her blouse and shoves a swollen breast at the sleeping Caroline.

As I discover, she does this everywhere—in the library, the grocery story, the gas station—oblivious to the stares of small-town clerks and customers who are unused to such blatant motherhood. Caroline, fastened to the source, sucks, gurgles, and waves her fists.

Minna is making a statement. "I had her. Now she is mine . . . and I, likewise, am hers."

For the first time, I am an alien, lacking the words, the experience to bring us back into focus. When Minna disappears into her cabin I go to the lake and stand there a long time seeing my shattered reflection in the moving water.

V SUMMER

As June deepens, as meadow rue replaces violets and the lake warms, Minna stays inside with Caroline, holding her, crooning fragments of old songs. I am left alone to read and write while shadows shift and the sparrows leave their nest making way for a second brood.

I wait for her to come out one morning smiling her familiar

smile, but she does not. She is polite, courteous, and remote, holding the chains that bind her as if to let them go will spell an even greater disaster.

Today is hot and still. The kids whine, and I would like to. "Tell your mother I'll take you to the island for a picnic," I say.

They run off happily, as if they have noticed no change.

When Minna comes out, she is unkempt, her hair in tangles, her blouse spotted with milk and food. "You must be careful," she says, and there is anger in her tone. "You will, won't you? Promise me?"

The idea that I would be reckless is astonishing. "Oh, come on, Minna," I say. "That's kind of weird."

She stares at me with icy eyes. "I don't think so."

She is a stranger, a Minna I cannot, do not like. The feeling unbalances me as if the earth, itself, cannot be trusted.

"Minna . . ." I begin and then am silent. "We'll be fine," I say at last. "Don't worry."

"But I will." She wraps her arms around herself and Caroline and watches us go.

We beach the boat in a small cove, and the kids swim and splash while I sit, notebook open in my lap. No words come, only the image of Minna's face. I feel as if she has died, leaving me marooned with no one to rescue either of us.

I unwrap the sandwiches and the bottles of warm pop, having forgotten to put ice in the chest, something the old Minna would never have done. No one notices. I think I am going mad.

The kids take turns rowing back. They giggle, wrestle, drop the oars, and move the boat erratically. We take a long time, but there is no hurry. Branches of trees, leafless and black with rot, float beneath the surface and threaten our progress. I try to push them away, but they are deep and come crowding back. Finally I take the oars and bring us to the dock.

In front of my door I find a package carelessly wrapped in torn brown paper and tied with a piece of unravelling string. There is a note scrawled on the top. "Thank you for letting me see these."

Inside are my poems, stories, musings of five years. Inside is my life. I stare, uncomprehending. My life has been tossed aside like newspapers for the trash. There is a coldness like stone in my mouth. Since I am rarely angry, I do not recognize the feeling, only the hurt that has triggered it.

Minna comes to her door before I knock. Her eyes glitter at me from behind the screen. "I've been waiting for you," she says.

"Let me in."

She slides the door open, closes it quietly behind me. "Caro's asleep. Do you want to see her?" She is whispering.

I am tired of whispers, innuendo. "No," I say, loudly. "I came to see you. I want to know why."

She tilts her head. "You don't know?"

Uninvited, I sit on the couch in the room I swept and polished. The blue desk is bare. This is the room of a stranger.

"No," I say. "I don't know why. How could I? You've changed is what I know, and I don't understand any of it."

She paces in front of me, those long strides better suited to the outdoors. "You have things to do," she says, refusing to look at me. "You don't need me anymore. So I'm setting you free to try your wings."

I sit with my hands between my knees and try to think rationally. One of us must. "How can you do that? Set me free? You don't own me. You're my friend."

How can I sound so calm faced with such illusions? I am not even sure whose illusion it is, or whether what is happening is reality and all that has gone before a dream.

"I know," she says, her voice small. "I know."

"Well, friendships don't just stop for no reason. Nobody decides somebody else's life and friendships for them."

She whirls on me. "That's just what I'm doing. You don't need me. You just think you do. Now please just go and leave us alone." She swoops down on Caroline who has begun to cry, and she holds her as if she thinks I will steal her. "You see?" she says. "You see?"

I do not see. I want to tell her that friendship is the sharing of needs. I want to take her hand and lead her into the sunlight, to force her to speak. I want to save her from something I can't understand, I want to keep her, but I have lost her, and the loss is harder for me, taken unawares, than for her who plotted the severance.

I open the door and run out, and I do not look back although I know she is watching, the baby at her breast, the sound of my footsteps final in her ears.

VI WINTER

Freedom is, of course, a dangerous thing. Given it I am adrift like a rowboat. I catch on snags, run aground, stare at the walls of my kitchen, and mourn my losses. I write, filling notebooks with questions that have no answers, with remembrances of sunsets, blackbirds, lush fringes of leaves beside deep water.

Peter returns to the lake without me. When he comes home he swears he will never go again. Martin, he says, has become like Minna—obsessed, erratic, impossible to work with. And so we are both adrift, deprived of our source, our work. We come together, clash, and part.

"Who are you?" I ask him in the dark, our bodies, our souls unmoored. "I don't know who you are."

"I don't know who you are, either," he says, and I can feel his indignation, as if I have cheated him.

Guilt, that ever-present hydra, rises out of my bones. "Why?" I ask. "What did I do?"

He moves away as everyone seems to move away from me lately.

"It's like I don't matter," he says bitterly. "As if all you care about is yourself. It's my work that's important, that's been ruined. Not yours."

"It's my work, too," I say, still humble. "It's me. It's what I am. And it's my friend that's gone. That's important, too. Can't you see?"

"No. No, I can't." He rolls over and lies with his back to me, a rock I cannot shatter, a stranger I have no wish to touch.

It is possible that we never knew one another; that what held us together was our lack of identity; that we were bound, as roots and vines are bound, beneath the torpor of the swamp. Now, denied place, we face our separate realities and flee in terror of ourselves. We are on our own. I have no comfort for either of us.

"Let him go," I think, unwillingly echoing Minna. "Let us both try our wings."

VII SPRING

"You have things to do." Minna's words follow me through deserted rooms, through the maze of my mind.

Yes, there are things I must do, a life I must live, write about. But it is my life and no other's, and as yet I do not understand it.

The interior of self is a chiaroscuro—darkness and light, strengths and flaws. I stay submerged in my own depths a long time, questioning the innocence upon which I built a world.

Simultaneously I am packing up the house, keeping or discarding objects and the resultant memories, touching with reverence or, now and then, distaste.

I begin in the attic, with baby clothes, letters, old shoes, baseball bats, shell collections, a book of pressed flowers, family photographs.

There Peter and I are on our honeymoon. We are standing in front of a Welsh castle and we are smiling, or Peter is. I seem dazed, as if I have stepped over a precipice and am hanging by a thread. Here the boys, a careful recording of their years from infancy to jubilant adolescence. And here I am with them beside the lake, all laughter erased from my face.

There are no photographs of Minna. I need none. Her voice is clear. "You have to write. Try . . . try . . . try . . ."

I pick up a stone fragment from a fossil collection. In it an insect is trapped in yellow amber. Others, minute creatures—fish on the verge of transformation, etched shapes possessed of both gills and lungs, fins and stumps of feet—compete for my attention.

I have seen dragonflies wriggling from the mud houses they

entered as fierce, sucking nymphs; have watched, spellbound, as the now-metamorphosed insect clutches the nearest stem and, in the rippling marsh light dries then spreads its stained-glass wings. I have seen so many maiden voyages, have tasted joy, have touched for one, solitary moment the continuity of the world.

This is what they felt! I tell myself, staring at the delicate filaments preserved in glass. This impulsion toward air, toward life and speech, for what reason neither they, nor we, now know.

But what I do know is that passion drove them. That screaming they lifted themselves out of the dark and drove toward consciousness. That leaping through millennia, some of them emerged into light.

THE LABORER IN THE VINEYARD

HILDA LOVE had never forgiven her daughter Marian for marrying a Jew. Not that David was a bad husband or father, and not that Hilda was a bigot. Some of her best friends were Jews.

The hurt lay deeper than that, so deep that she could not examine it, but it had to do with her own roots, her veneration of the solace of prayer, ritual, penance. She had supposed that she had instilled a similar worship of God and the Holy Church into Marian, along with the sense of propriety and the attendant guilt that kept men and women in their places, assured a smoothly run life overseen by a matriarch who answered only to God.

But Marian had been made of stronger stuff than Hilda had foreseen. She had renounced her early promise of curtseys, genuflections, reverence for saints and superpowers. She had not turned out to be sweet, malleable clay in need of her mother and religion, and these facts tormented Hilda when she thought of them which was often, for the more she tried to banish them, the more they came. The more she tried to reason (which was not her strong suit), the more her bewilderment grew, and her anger that she tried to hide, for Marian had a way of raising her voice and showing what seemed to be contempt that frightened her and sent her to her knees in prayer.

Hilda prayed often. For Marian, for David, for their two sons Richard and Simon, her grandchildren; little nonbelievers.

Hilda shuddered when she thought about them. She had, for years, prayed that blue-eyed Richard would become a priest, had been delighted when, in ninth grade, he announced that he would study Latin.

"That's wonderful, dear," she had said. "*Pax vobiscum.*"

"Huh?" said Richard.

"That means, 'Peace be with you.' It's in the Holy Mass."

"Oh," said Richard. "That."

Hilda filed this outrage away with the others, those things she would someday tell to Marian if she were courageous enough. Like the time when she had instructed Richard to kiss the crucifix of her rosary and he had looked at her and said, "Grandma, you've got to be kidding."

Marian had doomed not only her soul but the souls of her children, or she thought she had. Hilda, secretly and with great foresight, had baptized each one under her kitchen faucet when, as babies, they were entrusted to her care. Let Marian do something about that!

Richard had been a disappointment, though she boasted of his scholarly achievements to those friends blessed with less bright grandchildren. He was, at nineteen, firmly ensconced at M.I.T. studying the mysteries of the universe with Jewish scientists and not a priest in sight.

At this point Hilda would have turned her missionary impulse upon Simon, but he was as slippery as a fish, never standing still long enough for her to teach him anything. Besides, her husband Walter, who never went to church either, kept telling her to cut it out.

Hilda sniffed. "They have nothing to believe in. No guidelines, no source of strength."

"Cut it out," Walt said again. "Let them alone. You don't know what strength they have, and it's none of your business."

"Their souls are my business," she said. She also prayed that Walter would return to the fold, but with little success. She wondered why God had seen fit to surround her with infidels, to give her this cross to bear. And then she decided that it was her task to save them, to return them to Christ. Even young Simon with his brilliant smile and his schedule filled with tennis, dances, summer jobs.

"You wonder where they get all the energy," she said to Rose, David's mother one day. The two women were sitting in Marian's garden, Hilda out of a sense of duty, and Rose because she had moved into Marian's guest room and refused to move out.

"The Jewish Princess," Hilda had said to Marian at the time. "Now you'll find out what you married."

"Princess my foot!" snapped Marian. "Attila the Hun!" She stormed out, got a job, hired a maid to cater to the old woman's demands. The maid quit. So did the next three.

"She's impossible," said Marian. "She's never satisfied."

"She's old," said Hilda. "She's afraid to die."

"So am I," Marian retorted. "So am I. And if I were her I'd be twice as afraid."

To make up for her daughter's callousness, Hilda paid her duty calls, at first daily, then less often. Although she hated to admit it, Marian was right. Rose was impossible.

She was being impossible now. "You," she said to Hilda, "what do you know about energy? Here I am dying, and does anybody care?"

"God cares," said Hilda.

Rose laughed. "God!" she said. "Your trouble is, you never got out of this small town. In New York we knew better."

Hilda moved her plump shoulders the better to bear the cross. "Maybe that's the trouble with the world," she said bravely. "All this Godlessness. But I have my faith and it's a wonderful thing. Especially when you're old."

"You die," said Rose. "You're dirt, and that's it. The way I'm treated, I'm like dirt already."

"No one's treating you like that," Hilda said, wishing she didn't feel that she had to defend her own daughter even when she didn't approve. "You're here, and you've got your family. And look at this garden. When I was little I couldn't have imagined such a place. Let it give you some peace. Besides," she peered sideways, "you've got a soul, too. I know you do, and souls need beautiful things."

Rose tapped her fingers on the arm of her chair. She always tapped when she was bored or annoyed. "Why don't they stay home and take care of it, then instead of all this running around?" She tapped harder and got out of her chair with effort. "It's time for my nap and my heart pills," she said. She left Hilda in the garden to deal with the fluttering of her own heart at having survived the insults.

She wanted to cry but wouldn't permit herself that luxury. Instead she thought that on her next visit (not soon though, Lord, not soon), she would bring her prayer book and read those references to Paradise that might give Rose some relief.

Rose, however, waved her away. "Part history, part fiction," she said. "But you wouldn't know that."

Hilda went home and raged at Walt. "It's your fault!" she said. "You encouraged her to marry him in the first place. It broke my heart."

"Did you want an old maid? Didn't you want grandchildren? Doesn't it say somewhere to count your blessings?" He was reading the sports page and wished she would go away.

"I wanted another family," she said. "A real wedding. Baptisms and communions and all the little ones like angels. I did!" She cried as if her heart had, indeed, broken.

In a way it had. She had lost the dream that had sustained her all her life, and with it a part of her own faith, though that she would never admit. How could you say to God that His face had changed, that He had withdrawn His beneficence? She believed that somewhere, at some time, she had unknowingly incurred His wrath. She labored now to regain her lost status.

Walt was never one to comfort when he thought the cause foolish. He thought Hilda was a child, though a loved one, and he treated her as such. "Forget it now," he said gruffly. "Tend to your own business. Forget Rose. She's Marian's problem."

"She's an unhappy old woman. She needs God's love."

"She doesn't want it," he said. "If she did, she'd sure as hell demand it." He got up and went into the bathroom, newspaper in hand. It was the one place where he had peace. He went to the bathroom often.

Hilda paced awhile in the hall. None of them could see. None of them recognized the importance of their immortal souls. After awhile she crossed herself and prayed.

Two months later Rose had a stroke. She lay in her hospital bed looking yellow and shrunken like a dried-up insect. Only her eyes moved. Sometimes they were bright, almost pleading. Sometimes they hated.

"What's she thinking when she looks like that?" Marian asked Hilda. "I don't hate *her*. What I hate is how she tried to run my life. And the kids' lives, too."

"You never let anybody tell you what to do," Hilda answered. It felt good to let out her wrath once in awhile. "Your trouble is, you're not afraid of anything. And you haven't been very nice to Rose."

"Every time I tried she wanted more," Marian said. "So I stopped, that's all."

"She needs love. Why couldn't you do what she wanted?" It was not so much Rose she was talking about as herself, and Marian knew it.

"Because I can't love on command, that's why," Marian said. "I'm not a trick dog."

"You're stubborn. Hard." Hilda put on her gloves with great care, refusing to look at her daughter. "Those aren't nice traits in a woman."

Marian glared at her. She had no intentions of groveling for forgiveness. "Never mind," she said. "I am what I am, and that's that." What she meant was that she would never cross the barrier between them; would never permit Hilda to cross.

They walked down the hospital corridor together, the plump woman and the lean, both of them conscious of being out of synch, out of patience. Hilda offered her discomfort to God. Marian sped away at the door.

The idea of Rose waiting and fearing death tormented Hilda. "What if it was me?" she kept thinking. She made little visits bringing flowers, bunches of grapes, a bed jacket from the second-hand store to cover Rose's bony shoulders.

Sometimes she sat beside the bed and prayed; sometimes she talked. She was a good talker who could go on indefinitely, and Rose was a captive audience. Most of the time Rose seemed to be dozing, but that was alright. Hilda never required responses to her conversation. She prattled happily and then not so happily. She even told Rose about her misery over Marian. The dark eyes looked at her then with a glint of humor, but Hilda didn't notice. She was caught up in her dialogue. After a time she confessed her baptisms of the boys under the faucet and was startled when Rose stirred and mumbled a painful sound.

Hilda bent over the bed. "What, dear?" she asked. "Headache? Here, I'll put this cloth on your head." She dampened a wash cloth, folded it, laid it over the sick woman's forehead that bulged from under uncombed curls. "There," she said. "That should feel better." She smiled.

Rose stared at her in horror. Hilda went on talking.

It was when she reached for the cloth to cool it a second time that the idea took shape, grew in her like a cloud that blotted out all else. Peace! Comfort! She could give them both! She, Hilda, could pave this old woman's way out of life with a single act!

She never hesitated but seized the basin, rose up like the angel of the Lord, and poured.

"I baptize thee," she said in a loud, clear voice. "In the name of the Father, and of the Son, and of the Holy Ghost."

Then she sat down again, her heart pounding. The room was quiet. The late afternoon sun touched the foot of the bed, dust dancing in its light. Rose lay, eyes closed, still as death.

"There now," Hilda said. "There now. Straight to God you'll go. Don't be afraid."

Rose didn't move. Hilda took that as a sign of acceptance and was happy. She gathered her purse and gloves and patted Rose's hand. "I'm going now," she told her. "Rest in peace."

Rose moaned but did not open her eyes.

On her way out, Hilda stopped at the nurse's station. "Better check on her," she said to the young woman on duty. "She seems a bit restless to me."

At Rose's funeral four days later, Hilda peered a long time into the casket. Rose's face was set in death, but Hilda assured herself that it had about it a look of peace.

Then she turned around and saw Richard and Simon, her darlings, each wearing a yarmulke. She gasped. They looked like little Jews. Like rabbis in their dark jackets, their seriousness.

"Walter," she whispered. "Look at them." She clutched his arm.

"Come and sit down," Walter said. Then he, too, put on a skullcap.

She put her hand to her throat where her pulse leaped like a lamb. "Why?" she said. "Why, Walter?"

"It's custom, for God's sake," Walter said. "Stop it now."

She sat frozen throughout the ceremony, sneaking quick glances at the boys. "Foreigners," she thought. "Little Jews." Tears rose behind her eyelids.

When the service was finished, when the mourners had filed out into the parking lot, she pulled Marian aside. "I'm not coming to your house," she said. "I can't."

"Don't worry," Marian said. "I can manage."

"I am worried. Worried to death. The boys! Those things on their heads! Are they Jews?"

"Oh, for God's sake!" Marian said, sounding just like her father. "Haven't you ever heard about 'when in Rome?' It's custom. You do it. Even Dad did it. The boys are boys. That's all." The corners of her mouth were pulled in.

"It was how they looked!" Hilda said. "Like little rabbis."

"Please." Marian's eyes were beginning to crackle. "For once try and behave yourself. For once don't embarrass me. For once don't act self-righteous. Whether you like it or not, the world has different people in it."

It was her daughter standing there tall and angry and telling her, Hilda, to behave herself. It was her own precious child scorning her. She felt her heart crack as it always did when Marian looked at her like this, as if she were a naughty child.

"You," she said. "You don't know anything about how to behave. You don't love anyone but yourself. I'll tell you something." She paused to catch her breath. "I baptized her four days ago. In the hospital. I gave her peace which was more than you did."

"You what?" Marian stood motionless, like a movie scene stopped in mid-action.

"I baptized her. With the water in the basin." Hilda stuck out her chin.

Marian laughed. She laughed so hard her body shook and tears ran down her face. It was the last thing Hilda had expected, and it hurt, she wasn't sure why. "What's funny?" she demanded, looking up into her daughter's face.

"You!" Marian gasped. "Nobody's safe from you. You hide under hospital beds with your basins and vials and scurry around saving souls. What about *them?* What if they don't want to be saved?"

"They'll thank me someday," Hilda said. "When they enter the Kingdom of Heaven."

"This is the funniest thing I ever heard." Marian took off into laughter again. "It's unreal. No one would believe it. You know that? Nobody."

It was the ridicule that hurt, and the blindness behind it. All that she held sacred and had hoped to pass on, to be remembered by and cherished for was being cast aside, reduced to foolishness, and by the person she had once loved best in the world, by the child she had molded and shaped in her own image and with total faith.

Now, looking at the woman that child had become, she saw that there was no resemblance between them at all, that their differences were so vast and so complete that never again could she hope to reach out with advice or cautioning words. Never again could she rest secure knowing that her ideas and beliefs were being carried on though she, herself, be dust.

She turned and went out through the swinging door into the parking lot. The light dazzled her, and the heat. For a moment she was aware of her smallness, of her own fragility, of the vastness of the earth that surrounded her, bore her down without regard for faith or love or the innocence of belief.

She stretched out her hands to Walter over the shimmering asphalt, over the distance between them that seemed so large she did not think she could cross it alone.

"Walter," she cried. "Walter. Please! I want to go home."

GLASNOST

ON THE MORNING of my fortieth birthday I woke up and realized I'd lived more than half my life as a robot.

I'd never done anything selfish, that buzz word all women my age were taught to fear, anything with meaning just for me, some spontaneous act like swimming nude for the fun of it, or disappearing into the woods for a week. I'd never spoken my mind to anyone—not to my husband, my parents, or my friends and colleagues at the university where I had, for years and without enlightenment, taught nineteenth-century literature to students as identical as a mass of frog eggs—students with faces lacking passion or character, much, I supposed, as mine was.

I lay in bed smoking and thinking and watching the bare branches in Jake and Cissy Devine's garden. Jake and Cissy were old friends who had invited me to New York for a birthday bash.

My husband was at an engineering conference somewhere in the bowels of the Black Forest, no doubt eating Linzer Torte and expounding theories between bites. My children were at school. I was lying in a strange bed contemplating the abyss and smoking which in itself was a treat. Lewis didn't like me to smoke at all, let alone in bed, so naturally I didn't. Like most women of my generation, I'd been raised to do what I was told, to believe that my husband knew best, and though I sometimes had doubts about the reality of such a belief, it was easier to conform than to rock the boat. My youthful brainwashing extended to the dictum that one didn't question one's culture. Doing so led to upheaval, chaos, uncivilized behavior which, perhaps, had led to my career explaining nineteenth-century mores to the children of the twentieth century. Cast in the mold of a Victorian, I had spent my life defending my image.

"You really are a jerk," said my constant companion, the little voice inside my head. "Forty years a nonperson."

"Oh, shut up," I told her. I always told her that. She bugged me without mercy, kicked, screamed, raged, guffawed each time I slipped untouched through yet another fault in the crust of my life.

Then I reconsidered. "What's this nonperson stuff?" I asked.

"Just what I said. What you said. All you do is exist and drag me along with you. What've we done that's fun?"

"We?"

"Yeah," She said. "You and me, baby. Let's take a slow boat to China or something. Let's let down our hair."

"Never mind cruises. What are we talking about?"

"Us," She said. "You. You're a dead bore. You bore me stiff like that Jane Austen crap you teach. Always so proper. Why couldn't you have gone through with that affair with old what'sis?"

"Shut up," I said again. "It wouldn't have worked. It was the idea. The romance. You *know* all this, and I'm tired of talking about it."

"Bull," she said. "Figure yourself out for yourself."

Then She left, leaving me to think about Eric, "old what'sis," a visiting professor who'd courted me, flattered me, even God help me, kissed me until I nearly swooned like the repressed Victorian I am. But the brief affair, if that's what you call it, ended with a kiss because I didn't know how to pursue it; because I hid my eagerness—hell, my starvation for someone to bring me awake—behind layers of propriety and ladylike flutterings like a heroine in one of those novels I knew inside out. To my sorrow. I had loved Eric, even if only in my head, and the memory still hurt.

"You would bring that up," I said, reaching for another cigarette.

"Life's passing you by and all you can think about is what other people think. What about what you feel? What you think?"

"I don't know what I think."

She snorted. "So what else is new? You don't even know what you *do,* which isn't much. You just perform like a machine. You know all the words, do all the right things, and I wish I wasn't stuck with you. I'd like some wrong things, some excitement for a change."

"Ditto," I said. "Get lost."

I got up then, showered, dressed, headed downstairs toward the smell of coffee.

Jake and Cissy were hunched over the long pine table in their kitchen, coffee mugs in hand. We'd sat up late the night before philosophizing about the meaning of life. At least Jake and I had. He is a great wonderer. He wonders about everything and looks at the world with a kindly awe that does not extend to his real estate business about which he has no awe at all, merely a shrewd and profit-making acumen.

"Happy birthday," they said together, and Cissy's round face grew rounder with her smile. If she is a nonperson, she doesn't know it. Introspection isn't her strong suit. As a result, she and Jake are a perfect match.

"Coffee?" she asked.

"God, yes." I plunked down in my chair and let fly at Jake. After all, it was partly his fault. "I had a horrible thought," I said. "And it's all because of what we were talking about last night. I'm not real. Tell me I'm lying."

"You're lying," he said. Then he looked at me. "Maybe you'd better explain."

I tried. But when I'd finished he just smiled, a kind of weary lifting of the corners of his mouth, and said, "Join the club."

We sat there staring at each other while the pale January light spilled over us and onto the table like a river without a source or a delta.

"Listen, guys," Cissy said. "This is a birthday, not a consciousness-raising session."

Jake ran a hand through his gray hair. "Yeah," he said. He looked at me again, cautiously, as if he were afraid he'd see himself. "I've got to go look at a house in Brighton Beach. Want to come along?"

It had been years since I'd been there, to the amusement park with my parents and my aunt and uncle. We'd made a day of it, and my uncle who liked to spoil me had bought me ice cream and sodas, hot dogs and popcorn, and endless tickets for the merry-go-round, the only ride I liked and also the only one without danger. Elbows in, heels down, I sat the carved horses as if they were real, as if I were, indeed, riding down a beach beside an ocean so blue, so dazzling, it burned my eyes, left a taste in my mouth I could still remember. The taste of happiness. Of brilliant blue water. Where had it all gone?

"Down the tubes like everything else," came Her answer.

I ignored Her. "I'd love to go," I said to Jake.

"Count me out," said Cissy. "I've had enough therapy. See you at the party."

The weather was cold, the air so clear I could see details on the Jersey shore. Roofs of houses, the sun on tree branches, the motion and shape of gull wings making purple shadows on the water. I stared out the window as if I'd never seen the world before, and the light stabbed at me with the cold purity of metal.

"Atta girl. Wake up and enjoy the day," She said.

The house Jake looked at was in a compound with a security officer who stood in a little gate house like a prison guard. He looked at Jake's pass and hemmed and hawed and said it was out of date. Then he went back into his glass house to use the telephone. We could see him, ear to the receiver, waiting. At last he hung up and came out. "Nobody there," he announced. "Sorry."

Jake got out of the car. "Of course there's nobody there. I'm supposed to *sell* that house. I know there's nobody there." He pulled out his billfold. "Here's my ID. Driver's license, social security, American Express. Look at me. I'm me. Do I look like a criminal?"

The guard chewed his toothpick and regarded Jake seriously. "These days you gotta be careful," he said. "Something happens, I lose my job. I got a wife and kids."

"So does everybody." Jake took a ten dollar bill from the wallet. "Here. If anything happens, come get me."

He got back in the car and we waited for the barricade to lift. "Let that be a lesson," he said. "You want real? Real is numbers on a bunch of cards. It's the color of money. Who you are doesn't matter."

I got depressed all over again, and the sight of the empty house didn't help. It sat in the center of an untrimmed, unloved garden, and its porch sagged slightly. It looked like an old lady whose life had passed her by.

It looked like my third grade teacher, Sister Lucinda, laid out in the front room of the convent so that her students could kneel and pray for her soul. As a eight-year-old, what struck me was how remote she seemed, how unused, as if nothing had ever touched her enough to leave an expression on her pale face. She was dead, but it was worse than that. She'd never been alive to begin with.

I was so frightened that I pushed my way out of line and out of the room, and was punished for disrupting the ceremony and forgetting my manners. "Ladies didn't push," they said. Ladies didn't do much of anything in those days except sit and wait for gentlemen, or armor themselves against such an event with hair nets and sensible shoes like those spinster aunts who, now and then, came for an extended visit, and who sat primly on the front porch watching traffic on the street.

"This is awful," I said as my life flashed before me. "I'm having an identity crisis."

"Retard," She said.

I looked again at the blank windows of the house. What would they say about me in my coffin, bland as a pastry shell? "Here lies

Daisy the Untouched"? What would my kids remember? Peanut butter sandwiches? Chicken soup? A lap and a pair of arms that kept the world away?

She wriggled like a fish. "How about Daisy the Obscure?" She asked. "There you go again with other people. What about you? What do you want to remember?"

"Nothing," I said, glumly. I was sunk in despair.

Jake came back shaking his head. "Let's get out of here. If the rabbi wants it, he'll have to fix it, and he'll want it for nothing. Let's go to the park."

The park, of course, was closed for the winter, the stands shuttered, the rides dismantled. What remained was a clutter of abstractions, fragile skeletons in steel silhouetted against the sky, unadorned and purposeless as wrecks in a junkyard. Litter blew over the walkways, fluttered around posts and girders. Tin cans caught the sunlight, and here and there, looking totally out of place, a blade of saw grass caught the breeze.

"I'm not up to this," I said. The place looked like I felt.

Jake was sitting, one arm over the seat, staring bemusedly at the mess. He had that look of wonder on his face like he was seeing something other than what was there.

"What?" I asked. "What? Tell."

"I used to come here when I was a kid," he said, not taking his eyes off the Ferris wheel tower.

"I loved it. The noise, the rides, the people yelling. And when I was maybe thirteen I saw this woman. This beautiful, lush broad." His hands made her shape in the air, a miraculous vision of fecundity. "She was so gorgeous I followed her. She was with a guy, a soldier, and they walked and held hands and acted like they knew something I didn't. So I followed, and then they got on the Ferris wheel—that one right there—and I saw up her dress. All the way up. She wasn't wearing anything, and it was the first time I'd ever seen a woman. There she was. Just for a second, like a door into . . ." he hesitated. "Into what? Adulthood? Promise? I don't know. Something mysterious, anyhow. And she was a redhead."

She snickered. "Men never grow up," She said.

I answered Her without thinking. "I think it's a beautiful story."

Jake looked startled. "You do?" he said.

I remembered myself, part child, part horse, riding the edge of the waves and believing in paradise, so filled with faith and hope that even the ensuing years hadn't destroyed my vision.

"It's something to reach for. Isn't that what life is? Reaching for dreams? And isn't that the trouble? We forget. We live in our houses and grow old before our time. We lose the children and lose faith."

He reached for the ignition. "Maybe," he said. "I never thought about it like that. Let's go walk on the boardwalk. You'll love it."

He was right. I did love it; the wide planks above the deserted beach, the water blue as a Wedgewood plate and as flat, as still, and the women, God, the promenading women, plump as cream puffs, sleek as cats, each swathed in a coat of luxurious fur, each with a smooth cat face peeking between hat and collar, strolling, undulating islands of complacency.

"What is this?" I asked him. "Who are these eclairs?"

"Nobody from Jane Austen," She said, causing me to stamp my foot.

"Oh, go away, for God's sake," I said. "Who needs you?"

Jake looked bewildered. "Do you talk to yourself a lot? Been to a shrink lately?"

"Never mind. Just answer me. Where did these wonderful women come from?"

"Russia," he said. "They call this 'Little Odessa' now. I knew you'd like it."

"Like it? I love it. It's like being in another century, another country. Like Baden-Baden or Marienbad."

"Not again," She said. "What's wrong with here and now?"

I ignored her, turning to look at the winter beach. It was empty except for seaweed drying at the tide line and one old man who had deserted his fellows, those who were taking their leisure on benches, each in a rusty suit, each with a newspaper, each with a felt hat shading his eyes from the cold glare of the sun.

The old man was feeding the gulls popcorn from a brown bag, and he had his face lifted, and his arms, and his hair flashed silver like their wings as they swooped and screeched and wheeled in narrowing circles around him.

The purity of his offering, the stillness of the sea as if it were holding its breath, struck at me. I was small again, and joyous. I was standing on the beach, my pockets filled with shells; pink scallops, purple clams, those glittering silver and gold confections called jingle shells, each a treasure given by the sea. From my own brown bag I was flinging popcorn into the air for the birds that brushed me with their wings, wheeling so close that I was sure I could fly.

In a moment I was running down the steps and onto the sand where I pulled off my jacket, my boots, my stockings. Behind me I heard Jake calling my name over and over in a kind of squeak as if he thought I'd lost my mind.

"Daisy . . . Daisy . . . Daisy." His words stuck together in a meaningless stream of sound.

"Don't bother us. We're busy," She answered, gleeful as a kid leaning from a roller coaster.

I hit the water flying, skirt hitched to my hips. The cold burned at first, and then I didn't feel it. What I felt was happiness, unity, as if I could stop time; as if I could pick up the sea in my arms, keep the color of blue, the figure of the old man, the vision of the women, plump and powdered, who lined the railing watching, nodding with a wistful understanding born of repression, even as Jake hurtled toward me bent on rescue.

What I heard was the voice of self, a joyful shout spun out on the wind. "Come on . . . catch me! Catch me if you can!"

And suddenly there was a ripple in the sea of women as first one and then another moved toward the wooden steps. Slowly and then faster they came, flinging hats, coats, boots in a great, befurred heap on the beach before joining hands and dancing toward me, stamping their feet and singing in a language I didn't know but understood regardless.

It was the language of revolution, and we chanted the praises of freedom as we snaked down the beach along the tide line, one perplexed man and an army of women, unfettered by any culture, any ruler, any foolish history at all.

PART III

WIVES AND LOVERS

WIVES AND LOVERS

MALCOLM POTTER fell in love with Rena Ferris one morning when he was a guest in her house. He knew the signs. They were unmistakable. He stood at her back door watching her picking red raspberries, and his thighs began to twitch. Then the tips of his fingers grew itchy and his palms burned, as much for the touch of her flesh as for the need to recreate her in stone.

Malcolm was a sculptor. He was also a lover of women, constantly swept away by emotions he never tried to understand and therefore never could control.

Not that he wanted to. Malcolm Potter gloried in love, in the bodies of women, in the polarities of tension created by their difference from his own maleness. At work in his studio, he liked knowing that a woman awaited him in his kitchen, his garden, his bed. After wrestling with chisels, hammers, and unrelenting surfaces for hours, he relished the softness of the female form, the warmth of living breath, the music of human speech.

A statue of Evelyn, his first wife, graced the stairway of a museum in Chicago. Letty, his second, bloomed in a garden in Florence. After Letty he stopped marrying. Divorce bewildered him. Recrimination and demands wrung him dry, made him grieve and stopped his work that was as vital to him as loving. For Malcolm, being in love was almost the same as drawing shapes out of boulders or the trunks of trees. Both were affirmations of life. Both were to be relished, worshipped, cherished in the depths of his soul. His bold female figures continued to appear unabated in public places.

He stood at the door a long time admiring the plenitude of Rena's figure, the unbridled energy of her red hair which, in despair of controlling, she had tied back with a ribbon, but which broke loose in a thousand tendrils radiating light.

She left the berry bushes and strode across the grass to a border of lilies, red, orange, yellow, tall as skyrockets, and she bent over them, murmuring as she cut the stems.

At that point, Malcolm moved. He had forgotten she was the wife of Tom Ferris, his best friend since graduate school. He had forgotten his status of honored guest, here for the dedication of his bronze victory (Anne Marie) in the courtyard of the university library. He had, in short, forgotten everything except the fact that before him a lush and beautiful woman was bending over talking to her flowers. He thought he had never seen such tenderness on any face, or such round and perfect arms. He forgot that he was often struck by female tenderness, that he nurtured an ideal of Earth Goddess from whose roundness all living flowed.

He said, "Good morning."

She turned to face him. Her eyes shone; she had pollen on her nose.

He trembled.

"Berries for breakfast," she said. "And real cream."

"Gorgeous," he said.

"Did you sleep well?"

"That bed should be canonized." His fingers itched in his pockets. "And you have pollen on your nose."

"Do I?" She grinned, he noticed, with her whole body, as if summoning exuberance from some glad well.

He brushed the pollen from her. "Do they talk back?" he asked, pointing at the lilies.

Under her tan she blushed. "Oh, God," she said. "Don't tell Tom, will you? He thinks I'm nuts. But they're so real. Like people. So alive. I tell them they're beautiful. I say I'm taking them in the house and please to bloom there. It isn't that weird, is it?"

Tom, he reflected, had grown dry with the years. Precise. Fussy. Removed from the world and the language of flowers. From the glorious presence that was his wife. He saw she was lonely. "You're sweet," he said.

The corners of her mouth deepened. "Men," she said. "What do you know?"

He realized that he knew very little. He had never spoken to a plant in his life. Or to a field. Or to a tree except as a block of wood to be cursed at, dominated. But, unlike Tom, he was ready to be educated.

"Teach me," he said. "Will you?"

She looked at him a long time, steadily, carefully. He felt himself being sucked into her skin, her pores, her yellow eyes; being possessed, seen down to the cracks in his soul. And when she took his hand and pulled him to his knees beside her, he thought he would die of joy. He had not been rejected. Not for his weaknesses which were many, nor for his strengths which were potent but few. She knew. She accepted him. He smiled.

She smiled back. "You're sweet, too," she said. "You are. Really."

That he was being seduced never occurred to him until a long while later. Even then he was not sure. By then it didn't matter.

"Look at this lily." She turned a slim stalk toward him. "Really look. You're an artist. You know how. Go down into it. Feel it. Taste it. What do you see? What is it saying?"

He bent forward obediently. He saw stamens heavy with gold arching toward him. They tickled his nose. He drew back.

"Come on," she said, her hand warm on the back of his neck. "Look harder. Let yourself go. It's not hard to let go once you learn how."

He slid down the throat. The colors changed. Yellow became pale green; patterns shifted, moved. He was at the bottom of a great and pulsing sea, drowning in light and shadow, in faint perfume. Minute insects swam there. Golden dust, shaken by his breath, sifted down and lay glistening. The songs of birds were far away. He could not move.

"Come back now," she said, her lips against his ear. "Don't get lost in there. It's very easy. Even in Chickweed."

"Chickweed!" he said. "That's ridiculous."

"It's not. There's a whole world here. Sometimes you need a magnifying glass to find it, but it's here. Every one is different. Every one is beautiful. Even weeds."

Like women, he thought. He imagined them: rows of broad-shouldered migrant workers in tomato fields; nurses with white-stockinged legs; Parisiennes with pointed breasts under brilliant tunics; stark nuns, faces and hands; the Danae and Jupiter descending. Each in some way beautiful. Each a flower with a secret heart.

After the shadowed world of the lily, the sunlight hurt his eyes. He blinked. She swam before him, red-gold and laughing. He buried his head in her lap.

"Think of van Leeuwenhoek," she said. "Possessed, in love with all those puddles and sperm."

He shook his head, safe in the dark. "I don't want to think about him," he said. "I want to be lost. With you. Now."

She put her hands on his hair. He wondered at the ease of it all, at his surrender to a mystery which seemed, surrounding him, to be even more mysterious, to go on, spiraling, like the great curved petals of lilies that sprang from stalk, leaf, bulb, darkness of ground.

He thought she was trembling. Or was it laughter that shook her, spilling over him like the dance of pollen?

"Oh, Malcolm," she said, "you don't want to be lost. You want to be found."

It sounded so simple. As if, like Magellan or Columbus, he had embarked on a voyage of discovery only to find what he had always known; that he needed the delights of loving, and that he had, somehow, stumbled upon a woman who likewise needed, who likewise gave praise, but who voiced it differently, joyously with her flowers, silently within the walls of her body.

He looked up at her in wonder. Her eyes danced under the blaze of hair.

"Let's go eat raspberries." She put his hands against his cheeks. She looked mischievous, rumpled, as if she had just risen from sleep. "Let's eat raspberries and then," she laughed. Her fingers fluttered across his face. "Then we'll have the whole morning to watch the lilies bloom."

At the dedication ceremony that afternoon, he saw her, gracious and at ease in the front row. Tom sat at her side, erect, conscious of his eminence as University Professor of Medieval History. For a moment Malcolm didn't know whether to pity his friend who lived with a woman whose delights he had never discovered, or to envy him for the rapture that possibly awaited.

He sighed and rubbed his palms together surreptitiously. Deep in his studio he had kept for twenty years a block of golden stone, knowing from the first that whatever figure lay within would surface in its own time. He thought now of a lily, of a woman climbing, wanton, from within.

COMPROMISING ALICE

IN FIFTEEN YEARS of marriage to George, Alice learned to smile on cue, to make a perfect chocolate mousse, and to keep silent when shown her imperfections. Then she divorced George to marry Henry. Only, she told Henry, she had no intentions of remarrying immediately. She wanted space, breathing time, an interlude for herself to get over the shock of it all. She wanted, she said, to become reacquainted with the Alice that was in her, waiting to be born.

Henry acquiesced. Intelligent and fair-minded, he loved Alice for what she was and for what he glimpsed inside her, the shadow of another personality that had eluded all of them and that had, in the years of George's dominance, refused to die.

He helped her find an apartment on the second floor of an old house, and helped her move in, unpacking the china and glassware she had demanded as part of the divorce settlement, placing the furniture and rugs she had brought in the big rooms, and hanging curtains.

He had been, he realized, lonely for years, though he'd denied it to himself and his friends. "I have enough to keep me busy the rest of my life," was one of his favorite statements, and, though true, when he thought about it now it had a hollow sound, as if he were shouting to keep away the dark.

Henry lived on a small farm with six dogs, thirteen cats, an old grey horse named Loco, and a burro named Chiquita. When he felt the urge, or when he needed the money, he wrote mystery novels that sold well, paid the bills, and kept him in comfort.

Alice, who wrote for her local newspaper, had arrived on his doorstep one day in June asking for an interview. It had lasted all day. They sat on lawn chairs under the maple trees behind the house and talked and forgot about the time. The dogs came and went, the cats prowled and pounced under their feet, and Chiquita made hideous noises at them over the fence. Henry made an omelette for lunch, they drank white wine and laughed a lot. They talked about everything, men, women, animals, their own lives.

Alice was amazed to hear herself talking as if she had known Henry for years. She hadn't talked to George or he to her for as far back as she could remember. Not, at least, about things that mattered. They talked about George's job, about bills, repairs to the house, the defects in her cooking, and, sometimes, politics, when George told her whom she was voting for and why.

Henry wanted to talk about writing, about people, and most fascinating of all, about herself. Since no one had ever asked her about her feelings or cared what she thought, she was hesitant at first, but Henry was genuinely interested. She relaxed, slipped off the cloak of reserve with which she protected herself, and became, she thought, daring.

Henry had never married. He cherished his privacy for one thing, and for another, had never found the woman of his imagination.

"What's she like?" Alice asked, trying to picture the woman who could manage the menagerie, cook, clean, and be pretty and loving all at the same time.

Henry's hazel eyes shone with amusement. "That's what all women want to know," he said. "I'd rather not say."

"Careful," she said. "I could start this article with, 'Are you Henry Beeler's ideal woman?' Then you'd see something."

"Then I'd break that little neck of yours," he said. He smiled as he spoke, but her heart fluttered. He looked perfectly capable of doing it.

He said, "Women don't seem to know that a man likes brains." He was looking at her breasts through the thin silk of her blouse.

"Most men don't know how to show it then." She stared at him, resisting the urge to draw her collar closed, until, unembarrassed, he lifted his eyes and grinned.

"Oh," she said to herself. "This is getting dangerous." She squelched the thought on the instant. Henry was making no advances. He was sitting firm in his chair, and the light in his eye was the gleam of the late afternoon sun, that was all.

She looked at her watch. Four o'clock, and she had an hour's drive ahead of her. She stood up, flustered, dropping notebook and pencil, and she shook hands, promising to send him a copy of the interview before it went to press, all the time wondering what she would make for supper, and if George would come home hungry and cross.

"Oh dear," she said. "George will be angry about dinner."

"Who's George?" he asked, the gleam still in his eye.

"My husband."

"Oh," he said. Then he grinned. It was a wicked grin, and it cheered her. "Tell him to cook his own supper. Tell him you've got serious work to do. Tell him I seduced you."

"I can't tell him that!" she said, and then laughed at her own gullibility.

While she was getting into her car, she began to feel miserable. Henry was telling her the quickest way to the interstate and looking at her as if he were worried about her, and the feeling came. She didn't want to leave. She wanted to stay here in the shaded yard behind the old stone house and talk some more with this large and pleasant man. She wanted to be with Henry.

Instead she slammed the door, started the engine. Things like this didn't happen. You didn't just meet a man and in the space of a day wish to stay with him. Life wasn't like that. Or was it?

She drove down the lane and found the interstate, she never knew how.

George was waiting for her at home and, yes, he was angry.

"It's not like you're earning big money," he said. "I pay the taxes on what you make. I shouldn't have to wait for dinner on top of it."

She wanted to cry. To get into bed and pull the covers over her head. To think about Henry. Instead she bustled around the kitchen setting the table, chopping vegetables, putting two frozen steaks on to broil.

"Steak again," said George. "I'm getting sick of steak."

Alice kept silent. In her mind the seeds of revolt took root.

Four days later she delivered a copy of her feature article to Henry in person.

He was glad to see her. He had caught himself thinking about her more often than he usually thought about a woman, had once actually laughed aloud remembering something she had said. The sound of his laughter echoing through the empty kitchen disturbed him. He shook his head and began to think through a plot for his next book, a device that had always worked for him in the past.

This time his heroine resembled Alice. She had short dark hair and large dark eyes, and she laughed demurely as if the sound amazed her. Or she listened, giving undivided attention to the speaker, devouring him with her eyes.

"Now, Henry," he said to himself.

The dogs wagged their tails at the sound of his voice and looked at him expectantly. "Well, well," he said. He gave up plotting and decided to go for a walk.

Then Alice knocked at the door. "Am I disturbing you?" she asked. Her eyes were glad and anxious at the same time. He thought she was a nice person to be solicitous of his privacy.

"No," he said. "Would you like to go for a walk?"

"A walk?" How proper, she thought. How lovely. She said, "Yes. Let's."

"Take my arm," Henry said, and she tucked her hand into his proffered arm, discovering that walking thus brought them into close proximity.

They walked across the yard, through a field, halfway up a hill. Daisies were in bloom, foaming around them like spilled milk.

"Oh," she said. "How wonderful!"

She broke loose and whirled ahead of him to the crest. From there she could see for miles. Grasses bending, the glint of a creek in the bottomlands, a multiplicity of leaves in motion, all green, a thousand shadings of green that flicked at her eyes, lightened something that had been heavy inside her.

"You're so lucky living here," she said.

"I am." He looked at the grass beneath the oak tree wishing he had had the foresight to bring a rug, a blanket, anything at all. "Sit down," he said.

She didn't seem to mind. She sat, folding her legs gracefully under her, clasping her hands in her lap. "You sit, too," she said, her face alight.

He sat down close to her. He couldn't help it. "Was your husband mad at you the other night?" he asked.

She nodded. "He doesn't think I should work."

"Why not?"

She shrugged. "Because he likes the house perfect and his meals on time. He's used to it."

"Tell him to get unused to it. Tell him you're good at what you do and this is the twentieth century."

"I know," she said, looking down at her lap. "But it hasn't always been."

"You look like a painting I saw once," he said.

She looked at him for a long time. Then she laughed. "Is it my mind that interests you?" she asked.

He was taken aback. It was her potential that moved him, the woman who came and went, promising things.

"A part," he said. "Does it matter?"

She shook her head. "No," she answered. "I only asked. For the record."

In the moment before he kissed her, scenes from her life flashed through her mind as if she were drowning or about to be hanged. She wondered at the ease with which she shrugged off George, marriage, fifteen years of servitude. And then she wondered why it had taken her so long.

Henry was not a man who threw his heart over windmills frequently or without caution. After a time he drew back and looked at her hard.

"Do we know what we're doing?" he asked. "Do you?"

She was caught up in him, in what she felt to be a great hunger masked by his concern. She saw herself mirrored in his eyes, held gently as if on the surface of a lake. She saw her blue dress, her bare arms, the lights and shadows of June moving across her.

"I think so," she said. "Or maybe it doesn't matter."

"It does matter," he said. "Unfortunately."

"Why?" Having been reckless enough to kiss and be kissed, she was stirred to further recklessness by her body's momentum.

"Because you might regret it later. You're not the type to live a lie."

"How do you know that?" She clasped her hands in her lap again.

"Because we talked a lot the other day. And I've thought a lot about you since."

"You have?"

He laughed, and his eyes lit up with the gleam she'd remembered. "Women are always looking for compliments."

"I'm not. It's just . . . I thought about you, too. All the time. For four days." She blushed. She'd broken the cardinal rule she'd been raised on. *Never tell a man the truth.*

"Did you?" His face lit up as if someone had placed a candle behind it.

"Honest," she said. "I thought so much I couldn't stop. About all kinds of things."

He raised his eyebrows. They made neat, dark semicircles above his eyes. They were beautiful. She had never looked at eyebrows before, and that was interesting. Everyone had them. Didn't they?

"I even thought about van Gogh," she said. "About how he said that art should exaggerate the essentials and let the obvious alone." She twisted her hands feeling foolish and vulnerable. "And then I thought about how maybe I've been going at things the wrong way around. Neglecting the essentials. You know."

"Yes," he said. "I do. Most of us live like that."

"Well, it's all wrong," she said. Then she giggled. "Then I thought about eyebrows."

"You what?"

"Eyebrows," she said. "Yours. They're beautiful."

"Good God," he said. Then he laughed, too, and looked at her more closely and found himself trapped in a field of daisies, in a woman's honest eyes. He reached out and held her, accepting the obvious as essential.

Their affair continued for a year. Alice proofread Henry's manuscripts and offered advice. He proofread her articles, finding fault here and there. They fought, apologized, and made love.

In an illogical attempt to assuage her guilt which was, as Henry had foretold, considerable, Alice invited him to dinner. The evening was a disaster. George came home late and was tired. He wanted peace, quiet, early bed. Instead he found Henry in the kitchen, a sherry in his hand, laughing with Alice over the dessert .

He and Henry disagreed on politics, business, history, and the university system. They snorted at each other across the dinner table and pawed the rug with their feet.

Alice wished she could go home, except she was home. This was her home. And that was her husband. And that fierce-eyed bull defending her and women's rights was her lover. "Ah," she thought. "Henry," and felt herself go soft inside like a soufflé.

Not long after that she asked George for a divorce. She did not tell him she wanted to marry Henry. She would spare him that at least. He called Henry "irresponsible," "a master of trivia." Henry called him "Napoleon."

"A divorce!" George shouted. "What will people think?"

"Who cares?" she said. "And you won't have to pay my taxes anymore."

They fought over the furniture, the rugs, the china, and the quilts. They sold the silverware to pay the legal fees, and agreed to split the profits from the house.

When George had gone, the house was quiet. Empty. She came and went as she pleased, worked and ate when she felt like it. In the solitude something inside her expanded. She felt precise, grown-up, at ease with herself. She changed her hairstyle. Dined with friends George hadn't liked and she hadn't seen for years. She ate potato chips in bed and never noticed the crumbs. And she spent weekends at Henry's without any guilt at all.

One morning she woke up and saw herself in the mirror over the sink. It was an eager face that looked back at her, not the diffident image she had grown so used to she hardly noticed. She liked what she saw, and she hadn't liked herself in years. She brushed her teeth and flossed. She had never done that before. No time. George had wanted his breakfast on the table when he appeared.

Perhaps Henry would want the same. Perhaps Henry scattered his laundry around, too, and complained about holes in his socks and dust balls under the bed. Perhaps he, too, would demand attention to the obvious and forget the necessities, the need for warmth and caring. Perhaps once again she would have to compromise all that she was and felt. The thought frightened her. Getting used to someone was so difficult. Even getting used to her new self was difficult.

She made up her eyes, lingering over the mascara. That, too, was new. She batted her lashes slowly. She was pretty. She smiled. Henry would have to wait. Freedom was such a heady thing.

Henry was upset by her decision to rent an apartment but said nothing. He loved her and knew he might lose her by asserting rights or desires. She wanted time, needed it. Better for her to discover who she was and what she wanted now. He knew he was taking a chance, but what else was there to do?

Six months later when he entered her apartment with his key, he was nearly knocked off his feet by something he thought was a bloodhound.

"Surprise!" said Alice.

"Sort of," he said, brushing his trousers. "What is it?"

"Bloodhound," she said. "His name's Sambo."

"Rather inappropriate name, isn't it?"

"That's why," she said. "I bought a camper, too."

He went to the bar and poured himself a Scotch, straight. He had the feeling he'd need it. "What are you up to?"

"I'm going to drive across the country. Do a Steinbeck-type thing, only from a woman's point of view. You know. 'Travels With Sambo.' "

He choked. "You're crazy," he said. "Why do I want to marry you?"

"You said you liked women with brains," she reminded him. "I thought you'd be pleased."

He put down his drink and looked at her. She was barefoot, dressed in jeans and an old shirt. She was painting the kitchen ceiling and had spatters on her nose and across her cheeks. He wanted to seize her, carry her off to the bed, bury his face in her breasts and roar and beat his own chest and declare her his once and for all.

Instead he walked to the couch and sat down. "Come here," he said in the no-nonsense voice he used with his dogs.

She did.

"Sit," he said.

She did.

"Now," he said, "I want to ask you one thing."

She raised her eyebrows. "What?" she asked, breathless as a girl.

"How long do you expect me to wait?"

"Oh," she said. She dropped her eyes. "I don't know. I hadn't thought. I mean . . . I thought you'd want me to do it."

"Why should I?" He folded his arms across his chest. "Why would I stand here, give you my blessing, and cheerfully wave goodbye for God knows how long?"

She felt cruel. They loved each other and she was about to take advantage of the fact without considering him at all.

"I'm sorry," she said.

"That's not enough."

She pictured her trip as she had done many times. She and Sambo striking off across the plains, climbing the mountains like true pioneers. Then she thought of the farm, the stone house, the worn couch by the fireplace, the yard where the maples grew together with Henry's presence somehow weaving all into a welcoming whole.

"You could come, too," she said.

"I could."

She thought about George. His three-minute egg, his two-minute toast, his panic at the sight of a dust ball beneath the bed. She thought of being awakened at two in the morning and told about it, and about who would pay the taxes on her salary.

"Do you think you could make your own breakfast?" she asked.

"I've been doing it for years," he said, "why?"

"I mean, would you make me do it? I'm not too swift in the morning. I like to think a lot."

"I guess not." He gave up his idea of the two of them, heavy-eyed and warm from bed, waking over coffee at his kitchen table. "Not if you don't want to."

"And socks," she said. "I can't sew socks. Or buttons, either."

He shrugged.

"And if I have to go out on an assignment and am late for dinner, will you yell at me?"

He lost patience. "You," he said, "can sit here forever making up lists. The point is, you give a little, you get a little. I'm not perfect, and I suspect you aren't, either, but I'm not George. What do you want me to do? Get down on my knees, which I won't, or let you go, which I don't want to do either?"

She sighed. Freedom was so elusive. So short-lived. And what was it anyway? Was it getting up in the morning alone with time to primp, satisfying one's self without a thought of any other? Or did it all come down to a matter of adjustment, of compromise because you wanted something more than idle conversation with yourself, the going out and coming back to four walls and solitude?

Henry had stood by her while she crawled and learned to walk.

When she needed him, he had been there, was here now ready to catch her should she fall, his own fears not as hidden as he supposed.

She had come this far, for herself and for him, and he had waited, never wavering, and she loved him, although she doubted that was the correct word. He was an essential. For that you did what he asked. You gave a little and you got a lot. More than you deserved. You got a friend, a lover, laughter and talk and a meadow of flowers to walk in. You got the necessities the heart craved in exchange for mopping the dust, cooking the yellow eyes of eggs that made you ill to look at. And all it took was courage.

She touched his cheek. It was taut, waiting for her answer.

"We could go together and call it a honeymoon," she said.

BEFORE I HAVE TO GO

EMILY AND ROGER were sitting on Roger's porch drinking sherry. Emily was, for the moment, lost in a study of Roger's hand curled around the delicate glass, and in the way the color of the sherry deepened in the October light.

Roger was watching the effect of that same light on Emily's hair which had the sheen and color of horse chestnuts and which, an hour earlier, had been tangled upon his pillow.

She did not, he was thinking, look the least bit wanton. No one, seeing her there, would ever associate her with adultery or with the innate and unselfconscious sensuality that, even now after a year, caught him always off guard and unprepared. She looked and was self-contained, logical, capable. She was tall and appeared thinner than she was. Her movements had a certain tomboyish independence that rebuffed all possible offers of chivalry or familiarity. But something in the shape of her small shoulders, perhaps only the way she held them when she was tired or dejected, roused in him the need to protect.

Her shoulders were what he had first noticed about her as she sat beside the lake on a day much like this one. Only it had been morning then, and she had been sitting on a stone, her chin in her hand, her neck bending on its stem above shoulders so vulnerable he had stopped in his walk and moved across the pebbled beach toward her.

His dogs had been quicker. Spotted and black, and red as foxes, they had rippled around her, pawing at her jeans, snuffling at her ears. She had not rebuffed them as most women would have, but had opened her arms wide and gathered each one to her for a kiss and a hug saying, "Yes," and "Hello," and "Good dog," and laughing.

To him she said, "What wonderful dogs," as if she had known him all her life, as if she had been waiting for him on her stone beside the quiet lake and was not in the least surprised by his appearance.

That nothing ever surprised her he was to find out by degrees. That she accepted his arrival in her life at a time when he was needed, he was also to discover. He was a gift, she had said when, a week later they had kissed, embraced, and kissed again and then stood staring at one another in wonder.

He was a gift, and gifts were taken, used, treasured, never spurned. It had taken him a longer time to see himself in that light. He had not thought of himself as a treasure for many years, nor had his wife, living for her own pleasures in the city.

In time he began to take joy in the idea, going out of his way to make her laugh, encouraging her to play, to scamper with the dogs, to think because he loved to watch her thinking; loved the way she shut out the whole world and concentrated, eyes turned inward as if listening to herself. It was similar to the way in which she made love, focused, concentrated, as if there had never been, never would be, for her, anyone but himself. For that alone he would have loved her.

Emily was thinking about love, too, but she approached her ideas through her body, that root system of feeling and memory. Roger had delicate hands for a big man. He held his glass gently, unaware of the fact that he held all things in like manner, even, she thought, herself. It was odd that after twenty years of marriage, after a life lived in the orderly way that she had aspired to and cultivated, she should so suddenly be torn by a need for fragility, for sensuality, for the nurturing power of a man.

She who had always seen women as nurturers had been stopped short by her sudden and inexplicable need to be tended. She saw herself now as a desert plant; one of those stark, prickly things that put down roots, struggle, and survive until brought to bloom by circumstance, by the advent of the gift of rain.

What was even more of a shock to her was that she had believed herself to be content, even happy in her life before Roger. She had grown accustomed to her marriage to a neurosurgeon who was, literally, never with her even when he was. She had grown used to being alone, confiding her feelings to no one, her thoughts to a journal which more and more had become her friend, her support. Life, she had come to believe, was adjustment, and if moments of joy were few and far between, well, no one had ever promised heaven, at least no one in whom she believed.

It had become her custom to spend weeks at a time at the house on the lake that she and Mark had built when the twins were young and had needed the freedom of forest and water. Mark, she knew, did not really miss her except in isolated moments of physical hunger, and the twins were off in college.

She found the solitude of the country appealing, the lack of constraint welcome. She dressed in jeans, in shirts outgrown by the boys, and she rose early, walked, dreamed, existed in herself, content in the cycles of woodland and field. Women, she thought, were tied to the patterns of earth. They grew, fruited, were plucked, and grew barren. There was a certain comfort in the idea, as if she, who had indeed born the fruit of her body, was an active participant in an unvaried and unending flow of life and needed nothing more.

It was what she had been thinking, not without a certain pang, that morning by the October lake when the dogs had hurled themselves upon her, happy, greedy for contact, for the outward display of affection that is the birthright of dogs and, as she discovered, of humans, too. In the onslaught of paws, muzzles, fur, she had recognized a greeting, not a threat, and she had responded to the contact with living bodies.

And she had seen in the man who followed them, and who had eyes the warm color of sherry in the sun, a similar openness, an acceptance of her there, caught in contemplation of possible barrenness, of her life yawning outward toward a great and empty plain.

For a week they had walked, talked, eaten together in one house or another. Their houses were about a mile apart. The path between ran across a field that, in October, was still golden, and then through a small wood where, if they were lucky and moved quietly enough, they sometimes startled a browsing deer.

Neither of them, she thought, had ever imposed upon or jarred the other's solitude. What had happened was that each had expanded to include the other, that even before the first intimacy, the first embrace in the darkness of the forest, each had become part of the other's consciousness. Physical intimacy had sprung as a consequence. It had been gentle, natural, and as much a part of their lives as the flowing of seasons. She had not expected it, yet, when it happened, it seemed to be inevitable, right, given.

What had moved her was the depth of her tenderness for Roger, and the extent of her own loneliness. She had not thought that she was lonely, or had never dwelled on it. When, after ten days she had gone home to the city, to the well-run and proper house, to Mark whose hands performed miracles on all save herself, she had been lonely, deprived of the sweetness of blooming.

She had endured for a year, sustained by telephone calls, letters, a few days scattered here and there; by a week in the spring at the lake, three more in summer, and this last, with autumn showering around them poignant and final.

She was restless, though she sat apparently relaxed on the old wicker chair sipping her sherry. Physically sated, her mind danced, spun off like the leaves that skittered across the weedy yard and over the still lake surface.

Watching his hands, she frowned, a slight tensing of flesh and muscle that he, watching her, saw and translated correctly.

"You're thinking," he said because he knew she was and because he, for the first time felt excluded.

"Mmmm," she said, coming back to herself with some effort.

"What about?" he asked.

She shook her head. Her hair swung, glistening, along her chin. "I don't know. Something I couldn't catch. It was about us. You and me."

"What?" He prodded her. Above the rim of his glass, his eyes were alert.

"You're so persistent," she said, a little cross. She hated having to speak before she was ready, before she had examined the thoughts that filtered upward like bubbles through lake water.

"You looked so serious. I thought I could help." She had never been cross with him, had always been gentle, responsive, open, a clear window that denied him nothing. They had had, he thought, a perfect union, a perfect year, untouched by quarrels, by the aggravations of ordinary day to day living.

"I hate winter," she said.

Because he knew her, because he had devoted much time to knowing her, he understood what she meant, heard loneliness in the sound of the word—winter—and moved to obliterate it the only way he could. He said, "I love you."

She looked at him but did not smile, did not turn radiant as she had the other times. She felt, instead, more isolated than before, as if his words had sealed up the week, marked it closed, turned off what was, to her, a constant thing, rising upward, filling her with a sure and steady joy.

He loved her. She knew he did, but perhaps she loved more, needed more. She thought of her house; the big, warm rooms, the fireplaces, books, comfortable couches; the paintings, china, linen. She thought of the dinners she gave for Mark's colleagues, the parties she went to, the days spent shopping for silly things bought only to obliterate what could not be obliterated except here, in this shabby male retreat, where trees and lake flowed in and out of the windows, where her body belonged as much to her as to the man who yearned over it.

"I'm not sure what that means," she told him. "You love me sometimes. When I'm here. I love you all the time. No matter what."

He put his glass down carefully on the floor and moved so that his face was close to hers. "Love doesn't come and go," he said. "When you're here, I show it. When you aren't, I don't. That's all."

"That's what I mean," she said. "I want to show it every day. I want to dance, to play, to be happy all the time. I want to run out on the street and shout '*love!*' I want to shout out your name, not treat it like some kind of obscenity hidden in the closet. It's not fair." She put her square, boyish hands on top of his. "It's not honest. Not to us. Not to them."

"You want me to make an honest woman of you?" he asked, teasingly, to hide the panic that he felt, that he had been prepared for in the beginning but had forgotten as the weeks went by, each one happier than the last.

She got up, paced the length of the porch, her shoulders drooping. The sight moved him; would, probably, always move him.

"I don't know," she said, her back still turned. "It's all so hard, and it wasn't supposed to be. It was something we needed. It was supposed to make us happy."

And he wanted to make her happy. That was the trouble. "I know," he said. He put his arms around her from behind and held her so she fit into him.

They had talked it all out in the beginning, undaunted as lovers have always been. They could not leave their spouses who would, they believed, fall apart, die without them. Mark in the big house, laundry undone, the twins home on holidays, patients clamoring for his attention. Mark at the checkout counter confronted by the price of meat and potatoes. And Marjorie who had her own series of affairs but who, nonetheless, relied upon Roger as bulwark, as provider, protection from a world she had never understood.

"We didn't want to hurt them," she said. "Now it's us that hurt. Either way, it's us. They get off scot-free."

She wished he would stop kissing her neck. She couldn't think when he did that, when she could feel him surrounding her, giving her the protection of his maleness, the strength of his arms. And she had to think, for she was returning home with only a thin, cracked shell between self and reality.

Leaves blew around them. The old afternoon light coming from behind and through the chestnut tree at the edge of the yard cut through her sharply. Her bones rubbed themselves on the underside of her skin like cats sharpening their claws. Pain drove her to speech.

"It's not them we don't want to hurt," she whispered. "It's us. We're so used to it. To compromise. To our whole lives lived out all dull and filled with our little routines, our little habits, our sublimations. We're afraid of change. We're getting too old for it." When she was alone she ate her supper out of the pot and read a book leaning on the counter. Or she walked miles gathering weeds and grasses, bits and pieces of stones and flowers, and then yearned over them. And she wanted Roger yet was frightened by the idea of change, of having to readjust habits of body and mind put there by another. Indeed, she was frightened by having to disrupt that other's dependency.

Roger knew what she meant and accepted the truth though it hurt him to think of himself as rigid, as old and set in his ways. And, though he recognized and appreciated the fact that with him she seemed to bloom, he could not visualize her any other way. For him, that other Emily did not exist. For him she was always the same; honest, loving, free with her thoughts and affection, laughing and swinging her hair.

"Are you going to tell me we don't really know each other?" he asked, smiling down at her over her shoulder.

"Yes," she said loudly, more because of the pain beneath her skin than from anger. "I am. We don't. We only know days. They . . . them . . . they know the rest. They're in our bones. They know our whole lives and we know theirs." She turned and nestled into him. "They *are* us," she said. "In some awful way.

They made us and so we found each other, but they're here, too." She began to cry quietly, her tears soaking through his flannel shirt to his skin.

He had never seen her cry, never associated her vividness with tears. "Don't!" he said. "Please."

She shook her head and cried harder, her shoulders shaking like the branches of the treet.

He was exasperated. Why did she have to bring this up now, after a perfect week, after an interlude of such happiness that he had looked forward to remembering it, savoring it, keeping company with it through his own winter in the city? What was it she wanted? Change? Marriage? Romance that never died though they both understood that it did, that it would; that marriage meant compromise, the death of what they had enjoyed? Why, he wondered did she have to turn complex, thinking and analyzing, when the love between them had been enough?

But then he looked down at her, saw her shaken and somehow lost, a child-woman whom he cherished. He picked her up, carried her to the chair, and sat holding her in his lap.

"What do you want me to say?" he asked. He dug for his handkerchief, found it, patted the tears on her cheeks. "Do you want me to say we'll get married? That we'll go through with it? All of it? Hurt everybody? Do you want to take the chance?"

She looked at him, at his odd-colored eyes that she loved, at the flat line of his cheekbones that her fingers remembered, took the shape of unconsciously. He was life's gift to her. She knew it. The problem was how to continue to accept him.

Why was it, she wondered, that as one grew older, one's courage waned? Youth, armed with blind and stubborn faith in self and life, loved without hesitance, accepted without pause, while she stood fearful, arguing the issues, deciding none.

Looking at him she had no doubt that he loved her, that he would do whatever she asked him to do regardless of the cost to himself. She could demand that they take the chance, that they begin again in middle age to try and prove life wrong.

Or them could remain, at least for a time, as they were and had been, each filling the hollow spaces of the other. It would mean she would grow old without him. It would mean they would die alone. She hated to think of that, of empty days with each of them remembering, thinking of what might have been.

Decisions, acts of duty and devotion all demanded a bravery she was not sure she could summon, a strength she had already spent. Yet what was required of her now was a double act of courage. She would have to live with her loneliness, hold love in silence in order to have it at all.

She sighed and put her hands on each side of his face where his bones spoke to hers, those traitorous, living things within that she had felt but had never seen.

Around them the light shifted and changed, moved perilously close to the dark yet hung on, gilding the five-fingered leaves of the tree, illuminating his dark head from behind.

"Could we go back inside awhile?" she asked. "Before I have to go?"

LA SIGNORA JULIA

He is young, well-dressed, and walks with a swagger. He carries a bouquet of red chrysanthemums for the wife of Philip Cage, the Nobel Prize winning physicist, Philip Cage, with whom he, Paolo Contini, has come to study.

Although Cage's reputation is formidable, enough has been reported of Julia, of the house over which she presides, to make flowers a necessity and not the mere formality of Italian good manners.

Paolo does not know what to expect, and the sight of the house, big enough for a family of ten, gives him pause, Surely he must be mistaken. He searches his pockets for the directions Julia gave him by phone. No. This place of wide lawns, clipped shrubbery, high Victorian windows is, without doubt, his destination.

Within it, Philip Cage, the temperamental and distinguished professor, and his Signora, Julia, who they say must be a saint (Philip's demands, tastes, whimsies are repeated, embellished by the Italians who dote on originalities); Julia, whose cuisine borders on the angelic, who paints sprawling canvases of fruit, flowers, vegetables, and sells them, too, keeping her profits for herself.

Julia it seems has developed a passion for travel; not the acclaimed European lecture tours of her husband but unannounced flights over her own country, into the southwestern deserts, the unpopulated mountains, and she goes always alone without husband or friends.

Ah, say the romantic and discreet Italians. Ah. A lover? Two? No rumor of such ever reaches them. Julia remains mysterious, a woman who has visited Italy twice and never returned. They remember her as quiet, sweet-faced, a child trailing in the wake of the even then arrogant Philip. Those who have seen her in America since say that now it is otherwise. She smiles a lot, they say, and keeps to herself. She entertains well, withdrawing at the correct moment leaving the gentlemen to their talk of quarks, molecules, the laws of order and disorder; withdraws to some world she carries in herself charmingly and without effort. "La Signora Julia" they call her, nodding among themselves, unable to attach adjectives to her elusiveness.

And so Paolo mounts the steps and rings the bell.

The woman who answers seems not in the least mysterious. She has the wide, disarming smile of many Americans, and the good teeth, and she shakes his hand with a firm grip, reaching for the flowers as if they are treasure.

"Oh," she says. "How did you know? That color! It's my favorite. Look, Philip, what Paolo brought." And she whirls in the long hallway, making him feel that somehow he has done a great deed, brought happiness by his gift, his very appearance at her door.

She goes off, returns with the flowers in a silver bowl, deposits them with a flourish in the center of the long library table. "There!" she says. "There. Now let me take your coat. And can I bring you something? A sherry? A scotch? Whatever you'd like."

The great Philip Cage is, for the moment, pushed to the background, a figure against the fireplace. He puts a log into the flames, permits his wife her scene, her moment center stage.

Paolo bows from his waist. "A sherry?" he says, his inflection that of a question. Indeed, he isn't sure what to say or to whom he should speak. But she is off again, leaving him with Philip who, proud of his linguistic ability and eager for practice, crosses the room, offers his hand, and says, "Buon giorno, Paolo."

Philip is at home in this handsome room with its fire, its paneled walls, its books and antique furniture. It is Julia who disrupts as she returns carrying a tray of glasses, swinging her bright skirt, her silver jewelry dancing.

She is tall, as tall as Paolo, as Philip, and has short dark hair touched with the same red as the flowers. Paolo has the strangest feeling that, though she is polite, quick to say the correct thing, she is not really here, that she has sent another Julia in her place who mars the scene, disrupts the room's perfection.

He is correct. Julia has spent the afternoon writing to her lover, he about whom no one knows, and she is still with her words, her thoughts, her sketchbook where the letter waits to be finished.

Nor does he know that Philip and Julia have had a bitter quarrel, at the heart of which lies Philip's fear that Julia's painting is taking her away from her duties in the house and, ultimately, from him and his work. He sits at the center of things, supplies the money to run his domain, and expects perfection and service in return.

"We used to entertain. Now we never even use the good silver. And you never dress up anymore." This is Philip an hour before Paolo's arrival.

Julia is in sweater, skirt, low heels. "Look!" she says, "you want me to cook, I can't cook in a ball gown. I'm me, anyway, not some model in a photograph. You want the good china and silver? Fine. Tonight I'll use them. But I have two paintings to finish. When do I get to do that?"

"When I'm not here," he says. He is knotting his tie, admiring his reflection in the glass of the old Baroque mirror.

"And when is that?" Her eyes thunder at him. "The six hours a week you teach your classes? Don't be ridiculous, will you."

He says calmly, "I'm not. But I have the right to expect certain things. To invite colleagues for dinner without worrying that I'll disturb you. Your art doesn't run this place, remember?"

It is an old argument. They have had it many times, and the

truth of Philip's words always stuns her to silence. She knows the reality of his statement even as she knows that her art keeps her alive. Yet it also keeps her here, in this house, with this man who calls it her hobby, who assumes that he owns her. She is, in effect, his whore.

"Go to hell," she says. She runs down the stairs, her turquoise skirt a shout against white walls.

In the breakfast room that is her refuge, where she paints looking out at the garden, she seizes her tablet, writes in bold, black strokes, "My darling, I am coming . . ." and hopes that she is not too late, that he will wait for her, this man who loves her, who believes in her, who has stretched her mind beyond imagining. Adam, in whose arms she has slept, naked and cherished.

This, then, is what Paolo has interrupted with his chrysanthemums, his good manners, his eagerness to learn from Philip. This is what he feels watching Julia sip her sherry, make inquiries about friends not seen for years.

It is, perhaps, something in her eyes, a dreaminess, an excitement held back, or in the way she lifts her head as if she is proud, as if she has just arisen from a lover's bed.

He looks at Philip. No. There is not that passion between these two. Long married, they perform, entertain. It is a play he is seeing, one that has been polished to a high yet subtle gloss.

He is excited by possibility, leans toward Julia in order to see her better. "You paint, Signora," he says. "What do you paint? Abstractions? Realism? What?"

Her face takes on life with his interest. "No, not abstraction. Flowers, landscapes, the things of the world as they are. That's the beauty of it. Their reality. How close I can come to it, to the center." She has put down her glass and gestures with her hands as she talks. Paolo is fascinated by their strength.

"But I would like to see some of this work. Do you have it here?"

The walls of the house are hung with old masters in heavy frames but none of hers. Philip is a renowned collector. He stands now. "Come on," he says. "I'll give you the grand tour. Julia's paintings are in the breakfast room."

She remains in her chair staring at him as if stunned or angry. Then she says, "I will. I'll take him. They're mine, after all."

He continues down the hall talking as if he hasn't heard. "Julia's had quite a bit of success lately. Two shows, one in Washington, and both sold out. Another coming up in Santa Fe. I don't know what she's working on at the moment . . ." His voice trails off in the distance. Paolo, uncertain of what to do, follows him.

Julia trails them slowly and then swiftly as she remembers her sketchbook lying where she left it on her drawing table.

The men are standing in front of her easel. "Here's one nearly finished," Philip is saying. "What do you call this one, Julia?"

"Chamiso," she says. And to Paolo, "It's a plant from the Southwest. This is in the snow, and I'm not sure it's right. I keep trying to see it, to remember. . . ."

And what she remembers instead is the warmth of two bodies lying as if grafted; snow that began in the night's throat and Adam saying, "You're cold," and rising to put another log on the dying fire, to cover her with a blanket, to pull her to him warming her body, the secret network of her soul. What she remembers is a stab of tenderness, a ferocity that blinds her to all else, a reaching out to a male creature who wraps her in his arms in the scent of pinon from the fire.

Philip says, "Is anyone else hungry?" and again she looks at him blankly as if she cannot make sense out of his words.

She takes her sketchbook, puts it into a drawer. When she straightens she is smiling. "Go finish your sherry," she says. "I'll start dinner."

Paolo looks back once. She is standing in front of her easel, her head to one side. But it is the fluidity of her body that he will remember, as if she is poised, ready at any moment to leap into air and vanish.

He will also remember the dinner, tell about it when he returns home: the pasta, the meat, the salad, the fruit and cheese served in courses the Italian way; the effortless coming and going of plates and silver, the light of the fire, the taste of the wine, dark like old wood, like Julia's hair reflecting the flames. He will tell how she laughed, and how sometimes it seemed that she laughed not with them but at words only she could hear, at conversations spoken elsewhere, a long time before.

She will remember it, too, the last meal for a visitor that she cooks, and Paolo's praise. "Perfetto, Signora. A dinner my mother would make."

She smiles, goes then to wash the dishes, to resume her written dialogue. "Perhaps," she writes, "it's genetic, this cooking business. A female thing. Or perhaps I spent so much time in my grandmother's kitchen, and she was always cooking. And I was always hungry. And perhaps my love for you is genetic, too. And my hunger. In my bones, my blood."

When Paolo leaves at midnight she rewards him with another smile and says, "Please come again." And he feels delight, almost blessed. He stands outside the house on the sidewalk across the street and watches the lights on the lower floors go out one by one, those upstairs come on behind closed velvet curtains.

Do they make love? he wonders, his Latin heart stirred by the idea, by two such dissimilar people joining, forgetting their differences.

In their Baroque bed with its spiral posts, with angel's heads looking down from the tops of them, Julia lies quite still while Philip moves first his hands and then his lips over her breasts. And then she moves, permitting him to enter her. It is all done in silence, a charade for the benefit of the angels, in memory of the young Philip and Julia, she sweet-faced, tractable, he proud of his possession.

When he has finished, she rolls down her nightgown, goes to the bathroom to wash. She does not return to the bed but goes down the wide stairs, a white almost ghostly figure in the dark.

In her studio she stands a long time in front of her easel listening, as if for the fall of snow, the crackle of logs, the steady breathing of Adam who sleeps beside her while the sky lowers over the mountains, the great plain of the Rio Grande turns pale, and the dried chamiso flowers quiver with their burdens of lace.

Paolo returns to his hotel and, eventually, to Rome, where they ask him, "E la Signora Julia? Com' é sta?"

He finds he cannot tell them. She is a presence, there yet not there, felt but only as one feels an atmosphere, a change, like seasons.

When he hears that Julia has left Philip, has, indeed, vanished, he is not surprised. He thinks that the last time he or anyone else saw her was as she stood before her easel, her eyes on the chamiso in the snow.

WINDFALL

"MOM!" Mary Ellen's face gleamed with excitement. "There's a man in the duck pond!"

Nell put down her pen with a sense of release. Writing to Price, asking for another month before returning home was proving difficult. The words wouldn't come to explain who she was and why she needed to be here on the farm where she'd been born.

"What kind of man?" she asked.

"A funny man. With a beard. He's talking to Turgenev."

"What's he saying?"

"I don't know. I was too far away to tell."

Nell pushed back her chair. "Let's go see," she said and followed the capering child out the back door and through the vegetable garden.

Beyond that the land sloped into a field bright with Queen Anne's Lace. The duck pond lay in its flanks.

"See," said Mary Ellen. "There he is."

"At least he took off his shoes," Nell said, smiling. A pair of worn hiking boots sat on the bank, orange socks spilling out, their color clashing with the blue of chicory and tangled morning glories.

"Good morning," she called to the man in the water. "Turgenev doesn't understand English."

He straightened and stood squinting at her in the morning sun. "Good morning. I hope I'm not . . . I mean, I didn't want to bother anybody."

"You aren't. Just Turgenev." She pointed at the sculling goose.

"Funny name for a goose," the man said.

Mary Ellen, who had been squishing her toes in the mud, giggled. "He's a Russian goose. Like the one in the fairy tale book. He's got orange feet, and he's magic, too."

The man looked at Nell.

"That's right," she said. "He's right on the book's cover, and he came out of nowhere. One morning he was here. The ducks ignore him and the Canadas fight him, but he stays."

"Your jeans are getting awful wet," Mary Ellen said, and the man looked down and smiled. He had a pleasant face behind his beard.

Nell smiled in response. "She's right. You're welcome to come out and tell us why you're in there in the first place. My name's Nell Hartman."

"Josh McKenzie. From the Research Station." He came slowly out of the water, the tallest man they had ever seen.

Mary Ellen squealed. "Mom! It's like the tree man coming up out of the swamp!"

"This," said Nell, "is Mary Ellen who is going right now to put on coffee."

"All weedy and muddy with his face covered with . . ."

"GO!" Nell ordered, and the child scampered up the hill.

Josh smiled again. "How old is she?"

"Eight next week."

"Did you mean it about coffee?"

"Sure," said Nell. "Sticky buns, too. But I'd really like to know . . ."

"Why I was in your pond."

"Right. Tell me on the way."

He picked up his boots. "I'm doing a study on Canada Geese. This morning I was hiking the canal and saw yours."

"They come every year. Same ones, I think. Mary Ellen calls them Lucy and George."

His laughter was infectious. From somewhere outside herself, Nell heard herself laughing, too, easily, happily, and she wondered at the joyousness of it. She never laughed like this with Price. With Price she was always on good behavior. She listened and talked seriously. She never, in fact, laughed at all.

The realization caught at her, a swift pain, and she shook her head in annoyance, strands of her fine, yellow hair fanning out around her face. From the corner of her eye she saw Josh watching her while his long legs covered the ground, matching her stride for stride. The fact pleased her.

"Then what happened?" she asked.

"Then I saw Turgenev. He's a rare bird in these parts. A Lesser White-Front. Probably blown off course or hurt. I can't tell. He wouldn't let me get close."

"Now am I going to be pestered by bird watchers?" She stopped and looked up at him. He wasn't as young as she'd thought. Her own age, with a gentle mouth above the beard.

He shook his head. "I won't say anything, but I'd like to be able to watch him awhile if it's okay with you?"

"It's okay," she said. "I didn't mean to sound rude. It's just that I came here to get away from people, get back in touch with myself. In the city it's easy to forget about places like this where everything depends on everything else."

"You sound like an ecologist," he said.

"If you call leaving nature alone being an ecologist, then I guess I am."

"I call it wisdom," he said.

It was odd how, suddenly, she heard things. Cricket scrape and water sucking shore; bird wings and wind weaving through grass; a long sighing like her own held breath, and behind the man's quiet voice a warning of change.

"Some men I know think I'm crazy," she said, thinking of Price who, when he arrived for one of his widely-spaced weekends, cursed mosquitoes, damned the crickets, lay wakeful in the shifting night silences and in the hush of noon; who somehow inserted himself between her and her surroundings so she felt lost, cut off from something as necessary to her as air.

"You know the wrong men," he said, then looked embarrassed. "I'm sorry. I shouldn't have said that."

She said, "Why not? You're probably right. But how often do we meet the right people?"

"Not often. And when we do, we should hold on."

She had been writing Price not to come for a visit when Mary Ellen had called her. Price who wanted marriage, who had said, "Sell the farm and act civilized for a change." And forget the planting, the growth, the harvest; the fox in the cornfield, the ducklings on the bank. Forget the picking of berries, the windfalls in the orchard grass, the frogs that sang every night long into darkness. Price, whose presence disrupted her as, oddly, this stranger did not.

"The men I know all see nature as a challenge. Change it. Conquer it. Cement the fields and fill the creek and never mind the old bass down there, or the butterflies. Oh . . ." she caught herself and, frowning, threw out her arms. "Why am I going on like this?"

She thought he would touch her. Lean down like a branch and take her face between his hands. And she thought she would not mind.

Instead he took the strand of hair that had blown across her cheek and tucked it carefully behind her ear. "Because you care," he said. "Most people want to change it. To leave their own mark. Otherwise, they're afraid."

"We're too civilized," she said, remembering Price and realizing that she would have responded to this man like any creature in its season, any fallow field that feels its emptiness and strives to bloom. Frightened by her feelings, she walked faster.

He kept pace, looking at her with genuine interest. "What do you mean?" he asked.

"It's like we have no minds of our own." She refused to meet his eyes. "No hearts. We're programmed to do as we're told, not as we feel, and so we fit into little slots and die."

His response was a laugh that sounded bitter, and another question. "And do you have a solution?"

A solution was what she'd been seeking and what had, so far, eluded her. She shook her head. "No. Maybe I never will. Now we've talked so long it's almost noon. Stay for lunch?"

"No trouble?"

"Nope. We'll eat what's there. Eggs and herbs. An omelet, maybe."

"And sticky buns?" Lines came and went around his eyes. She thought that, despite the momentary bitterness, he must laugh often, even to himself.

"Sure," she said. "Mary Ellen and I are champion sticky bun bakers. Besides, it's good to talk. I've been working so hard I don't know what I'm doing anymore."

"Working at what?"

"Finishing a book. And deciding what to do with my life." God! In a few more minutes she'd be telling him everything! And all because his eyes were kind, his hands gentle. Was she so needy that even the smallest attention reduced her to foolish babbling?

She squared her shoulders. "Come on," she said. "Let's see what Mary Ellen's done with that coffee."

During the next weeks Josh came and went, sometimes bringing the mail from the box at the end of the lane, sometimes a day-old newspaper from the city, and once a basket filled with wild strawberries he had picked on one of his hikes.

Sometimes he would take a cup of coffee and sit on the porch steps, back against the railing, long-legged and at ease. He did not disturb her solitude, but enlarged it in a way she could not fathom or even put into words, but recognized in an increasing awareness, in a heightening of her senses so that she heard things that had been peripheral, looked at her fields in a different way as if she grew in them and they in her.

She began to write fiercely, her words falling into place almost ahead of her pen. Sometimes she showed what she had done to Josh as she had never showed anyone, not even Price, and she thrilled to the fact that he understood what she was doing, made suggestions, accepted her work as serious.

She rose earlier, while the mist still clung to the hollows, and worked until she heard his footsteps or Mary Ellen's shout of welcome. She would see them, tree man and sprite, and leave her desk eager for their company.

On the days when he did not come, she worked till noon, stopped for lunch, and wondered why he had not walked the lane or the canal, or if he had, why she had not seen him.

He'd given Mary Ellen a bird guide for her birthday, and she had set out to learn the names and habits of every bird in the area. She often tagged along behind him, chattering and curious.

"What do you two talk about?" Nell asked her one night at bedtime.

"Lots," the child said. "He's told me all about the geese. Where they go in winter. Down to the . . ." she wrinkled her forehead, "the Ches-a-peak?"

"Right," said Nell.

"And how they marry for life. Not like people. Like you and Dad. Josh says Lucy and George have been married a long time. Six years maybe. Josh was married, too. Like you."

"Was he?" Nell hadn't pictured him married. He seemed so bound to the fields, to his solitary life.

"He has a little girl. Older than me. She lives with her mother."

"Oh," said Nell.

The pine tree brushed the eaves. In the forest an owl screeched and was silent. The night flowed in at the windows, and the moon.

She kissed Mary Ellen and went down the narrow stairs out onto the porch where her mother's chair rocked by itself, and the faint perfume of warm hay and sweet clover lingered.

She sat in her mother's place and remembered her own childhood here, on this farm. Here she had played, yearned, hungered for learning and for flight. She had studied, become a teacher, then a writer, then a wife and mother all in a steady flowing like a stream that knows its destination. Only she had not known hers. She had, she thought, made few decisions in her life, had just gone on doing what the moment required, what women had done for centuries. Even divorce hadn't been her idea. It had been Tom's, and she had agreed without argument. Not that she missed him. He had never touched her heart, had been a mistake except for Mary Ellen. Josh had the same honest qualities as the child, she thought. Open, honest, vulnerable.

Better not think about him. What, after all, did she know about him? He'd been married but hadn't told her; had confided instead in Mary Ellen. Why? She shook her head and wondered at her own indignation.

Better to worry about Price who was becoming petulant alone in the city, whose letters all bore a similar message. "How much longer are you going to isolate yourself? When are you coming home? Why are you avoiding me?"

She was avoiding him. She knew it. She was avoiding a decision too painful to face.

As if forcing the issue, a letter from Price arrived in the mail Josh brought the next morning. Reading it, she found she could no longer visualize him, could not remember why she loved him, or if she ever had. She had crumpled the paper between her fingers and stared out over the fields.

"Bad news?" Josh asked.

"No. I just wish I didn't feel torn in half."

He sat quiet for a long time, his eyes following the direction of hers as if trying to see what she saw. Then he said, "Life's hard enough without that."

"I know."

He was quiet again, but she felt in him a struggle, a sifting of words. When he looked at her again, his eyes were sad. "I keep thinking people are supposed to help each other. Mostly, though, they just tear each other apart. That's what happened with my wife and me. Don't let it happen to you."

"How do you know it would?" she asked, curious.

He shrugged. "I don't. All I know is that I keep seeing you upset. Think how it would be married to him."

"Why is it," she said, "that you and I always talk about things that matter?"

"Do we?"

"Right to basics every time."

He thought a moment. "You're a woman who doesn't need pretty pictures or frills," he said. "You're honest."

"Did your wife want those things?"

His mouth tightened in that bitter line she'd seen before. Then he said, "Yes. She did. She wanted everything. All of me. Some people are like that."

He stood abruptly and went off down the path as if he'd said too much, touched some inner place of pain. Nell wanted to call him back, to run after him to comfort and, perhaps, find words she could apply to her own situation, but, remembering the sorrow in his face, she stayed where she was and watched him out of sight.

For the rest of the day she thought about his description of her—a woman who didn't need frills. Price had said she was avoiding life, but was she? Was she not, instead, going beyond the surface to the greater flowing of seasons, migrations, realities? Was she not, perhaps, learning truths through Josh's eyes?

In the morning she would look out, see him with the geese or making his way down the path, and she would ask him to dinner and afterwards they could sit here and talk. It had been years since she'd spoken her thoughts. They had been, she realized now, lonely years, without companionship or the comfort of honest speech.

It was August. Already summer sounded old. Crickets rasped all day in drying grass. Birds no longer nested or guarded territories with fierce music. The scent of ripe windfall apples, those bruised fruits heavy with sweetness, filled the house.

"Let's make applesauce," said Mary Ellen. "And can some to take home." Practical, knowing the taste of summer stored in a jar.

"Alright," Nell said. "And while we're at it, let's ask Josh to supper. Would you like that?"

"Yes. He's my best friend."

"Better than Price?"

"Oh, Price," said Mary Ellen. "All he knows about is movies. Josh knows about snakes and stuff."

And that, Nell thought, was important. Knowing about snakes. Frogs that twanged in the swamp. Bees that worked the fields, their bodies gold in the sun. Knowing the basics. The music of earth.

"He's fun, huh?"

"Super. Did you know that water snakes will attack a boat?"

Nell shuddered. "No. They give a mean bite, though."

"We watched one swimming. It wasn't awful. It was like . . ." she closed her eyes, remembering. "It was like *stars*, Mom." Delighted with her description, she danced barefoot toward the door.

"Did you say that to Josh?"

"Sort of. He says he bets I'll be a writer like you someday."

"Maybe," said Nell. "If you want. But it's work, you know. Not just wanting to."

"I know. I know. I'll go get apples now." She slammed the door. Her blue jeans flashed under the apple branches.

Happiness. Here. Now. In the blue kitchen, curtains blowing in and out, spinnakers, sunbeams, visible pulse. Immediate, not stored in a jar to be meted out little by little.

"I don't want to go home," she thought. She said it aloud and shivered. Not going home would mean giving up the comforts of the city; libraries, concerts, Price, solid, capable, dreamless. Price who had forgotten how to laugh. Who saw her world as though on film, as isolated moments of which he would never be apart. Beautiful in retrospect, frightening in immediacy, as, perhaps, he thought of her.

It would mean autumn would be hers. Leaf fall. Mysterious migrations of geese. The cold stars of Queen Anne's Lace at the sides of the road. And the long snows, the white cold, ice on reeds and on the blue face of the pond.

It would mean waking a child in the dark, walking to the school bus stop before the sun rose; carting wood, sealing cracks, trekking into town for food and books.

"Well," she thought. "Well. No need to decide this second."

She'd walk to the pond and find Josh.

Ironweed was showing purple fringes. Early goldenrod leaned in the wind. She felt a sorrow in herself, an aching for the summer nearly spent, a need for reasons, meanings, something more than the minute selfish acts that shaped a day, made a biography.

He wasn't at the pond. She turned and walked the cinder track that bordered the canal. A buck broke cover at her approach, leaped, vanished without sound of hooves. On the surface of the water, spatterdock leaned into the current, lilies lifted with the wind. Where the water widened into a shallow lake she found him propped against a tree, binoculars to his eyes. She sat down beside him.

"Stay quiet a minute," he whispered. "There's a heron over there."

"The rookery is behind those trees. Haven't you been there?"

He lowered the glasses. "Not yet. Will you take me?"

"Sure. You should see it. It's like being in prehistoric times watching pterodactyls. And we don't even need a time machine."

"Mary Ellen says you'll be leaving soon."

"Maybe," she said. "I'm thinking of staying, but there are lots of things to consider."

"Like?"

"Oh, school. Being isolated. Making out in blizzards. I did it as a kid, but I had my family. Now there's only Mary Ellen and me. It could turn out to be a disaster."

"Could be," he said. "Or it could be it's what you need."

She slipped off her shoes, put her feet in the water. "How do you know what I need?"

"Because you love this place." He smiled at her feet, submerged. "You belong here and you know it. It makes you happy. What do you need with the city? With another bad marriage?"

Kitchen curtains lifting. The scents of water and fallen apples. "Happiness comes and goes. We can't have it all the time. We'd not recognize it when it comes."

"But you don't have to go looking for misery, either," he said. "Are you happy with Price?" His eyes were direct.

She could not lie to him. He deserved truth, somehow gave it back. "For awhile I was," she said. "In the beginning. But not now. He *wants* so much. And we pull in opposite directions. Price isn't peaceful."

"I'll be here all winter if you need anything," he said.

Would that make her happy? This male presence so like her own, yet different, so that she seemed to unfold, to understand mysteries she had locked inside herself?

Her nostrils quivered, scenting, assessing. Warmth of body, laundry soap, something sweet and grassy like woodland, something smoky like burning leaves.

"Do we choose?" she asked. "Or are we chosen? Do we direct our little boats or just get swept along? I've never known."

He moved and came in contact with the length of her body, shoulder to thigh. She did not pull away. In the water their feet touched, cool, like the coming together of fish.

"I think," he said slowly, as if hauling the words a long distance, "I think the choice is that of entering the stream or watching it pass. Of choosing to feel or not to feel. You can live with passion or, like you said, in some safe little slot where you die. Response is always choice."

A dragonfly came from nowhere, landed on her knee and hummed and quivered, its wings a gold-worked lace. Hardly breathing, they watched it dance, lift off, hover flashing above the water.

Joy rose in her demanding to be shared. In his eyes she saw herself, a fleck of gold and blue, a woman dreaming safe upon a bank while life flew by.

She leaned toward him, hesitated, then cast off into the invisible current.

When he kissed her she thought of divers meeting in mid-air, the cries in both throats silenced.

A NOTE ABOUT THE AUTHOR

JANE CANDIA COLEMAN received the Western Heritage Award in 1992 for her first collection of short fiction, "Stories From Mesa Country," published by Ohio University Press/Swallow Press. Her first poetry collection, "No Roof But Sky," High Plains Press, received the Western Heritage Award in 1991.

The co-founder and former director of the Women's Creative Writing Center at Carlow College in Pittsburgh, she now lives on a ranch near Rodeo, New Mexico and writes full time.

0 00 02 0564911 4
MIDDLEBURY COLLEGE